Four Secrets Kept

FOUR SECRETS KEPT

A Secrets of Hartwell Novel

H L Marsay

TULE
PUBLISHING

The human heart has hidden treasures,
In secret kept, in silence sealed;
The thoughts, the hopes, the dreams, the pleasures,
Whose charms were broken if revealed.

Charlotte Brontë 1816–1855
Yorkshire

CHAPTER ONE

I T WAS A beautiful summer's day. The sky was cornflower blue and there was barely a cloud in sight. Detective Sergeant Jo Ormond stood in the shadow of a yew tree, a little apart from the mourners. Lord Rupert Hanley was finally being laid to rest in the family plot in the graveyard of Hartwell church. However, unlike everyone else present, Jo had never met his lordship.

Standing by the grave was Lucy, Rupert's widow. Her tall, slim frame was elegantly dressed in black. Jo wondered what thoughts were going through her friend's mind. It was impossible to see her face beneath the veil attached to her wide-brimmed hat, but Jo could see her knuckles gleaming white as she clutched tightly on to the hand of her son, Freddie. The little boy was wearing a dark suit and tie that made him look far older than he was. His pale, serious face stared straight ahead of him except for the occasional glance up at his mother. On his other side stood Caroline, his paternal grandmother. Although she wasn't wearing a veil, her expression was just as impossible to read as her daughter-in-law's.

Jo's eyes scanned the rest of the mourners as Reverend Davenport continued to address them in his ponderous monotone. Surrounding Lucy, Caroline and Freddie were a collection of smartly dressed men and women with similar hawklike features that Jo took to be other members of the Hanley family. Lined up opposite them were villagers, local dignitaries and tenants of the Hartwell estate. They had all come to pay their final respects to a man Jo knew many of them disliked.

Nora Parkin, the local shopkeeper and village busybody, had elbowed her way to the front of the mourners and was straining her neck to read all the notes attached to the many floral tributes. Rob Harrison, the local boy who had returned to Hartwell after making a fortune in property stood at the edge of the group. His handsome, chiselled features were impassive, but Jo noticed his deep blue eyes remained firmly fixed on Lucy.

Rachel, a teacher at the village school and Lucy's best friend, was standing alongside her mother, Mary. With her brown hair tied in a long plait down her back, her face looked pale and drawn and there were dark circles beneath her eyes. They were surrounded by other members of the vast Foxton clan. Their family had been farming in the village for centuries.

The only Foxton who wasn't part of the group was Becky, Rachel's sister. She was married to Max—the agent who worked for the Hartwell estate. They had positioned themselves behind the Hanleys on the other side of the grave, clearly hoping to blend in with the aristocracy. Max was the biggest social climber Jo had ever met. He even tried to turn the flat vowels of his Mancunian accent into an upper-class drawl. It was probably just as well he and Becky weren't standing near Rachel. There certainly wasn't any love lost between the two sisters.

Colonel Marsden, the retired soldier and head of the parish council, stood to attention directly opposite Caroline and Lucy. The medals attached to his chest glinted brightly in the sun. Jack, the burly, bear-like landlord of the White Hart was standing between the colonel and his mother, Shirley, who had dyed her hair jet black in honour of the occasion. As soon as Jack had spotted Jo, he'd smiled and beckoned her over to join them. She'd shaken her head and remained under the tree. She was an outsider. She didn't really belong here, but professional curiosity had got the better of her.

Rupert had disappeared on the night of the first lockdown, but his remains were only discovered a few weeks ago in a cave on the moors. Jo had hoped investigating his death and finding his killer might have been her ticket out of North Yorkshire and back to the metropolitan police. However, the coroner had returned an open verdict and her superiors had informed her that the case was closed. Jo was certain Rupert hadn't died of an overdose as most people seemed to think, but she was starting to doubt if she'd ever find out the truth. Hartwell might appear to be a sleepy, quaint little village nestled between the moors and the dales, but if Jo had learnt one thing since she'd been here, it was that Hartwell's inhabitants were very good at keeping secrets.

As the Rev continued to drone on, Jo stepped farther back into the shade and leaned against the large headstone that marked the final resting place of Joseph Baxter Tarrant, a young archaeologist who had died nearly thirty years ago. She began to absent-mindedly fiddle with the silver coin pendant that she always wore around her neck. Since Jack had told her the story of the Hartwell nobles, she'd found herself thinking about it more than she had in years.

According to legend, the coins had been minted and presented to local families to try and lift a curse that had plagued the Hanley family since they built Hartwell Hall on sacred Druid land. It was the only thing she'd been left with when she was abandoned as a baby, and Jack was convinced it must mean she had some sort of connection to Hartwell. Letting her eyes travel away from the mourners and wander over the old moss-covered gravestones, she wondered if some of her own ancestors might be buried here. Then she gave her head a firm shake. She didn't like dwelling on her past; it did no good. The funeral must be getting to her more than she'd thought.

Finally, Reverend Davenport finished speaking. Jo watched as Caroline bent down and with a gloved hand picked up some earth and, after the briefest pause, tossed it onto the coffin. Lucy followed her before helping Freddie to do the same. Then the three of them turned and slowly made their way past the floral tributes and down the path to the waiting cars. The other mourners waited a few moments before drifting after them. They spoke in hushed, respectful tones, but Jo noticed that not one of them had shed a tear.

She waited until they had all left the churchyard and watched as the gravediggers appeared and began shovelling the earth over the coffin. The soft rhythmic thuds combined with the wood pigeons cooing in the trees and the bees buzzing around the flowers. To Jo the countryside could be every bit as noisy as London. This was the longest she'd been away from her home city, and the way things were going it didn't look like she would be returning anytime soon.

"Jo? Why are you here? Has something happened?"

Jo spun around. She'd thought she was alone, but Rachel was standing behind her. She must have come back.

"No. Nothing," said Jo, quickly. "The chief constable thought the police should be represented, so I volunteered, but I didn't want to intrude." This wasn't strictly true, but then Rachel hadn't always been totally honest with her either.

"So, the investigation is definitely over? It hasn't been reopened?" Rachel persisted, her face full of concern.

"Yes, I told you," replied Jo lowering her voice. "There is nothing for you and Lucy to worry about."

Rachel studied her for a second, then nodded.

"Are you going up to the Hall?" she asked, sounding a little more relaxed.

Jo shook her head.

"No, I have to get back to work. What about you?"

"No. I'm going to take Mum home. I've left her talking to Jack and Shirley, but she seems a bit upset. I think today has brought back memories of when we buried Dad." She nodded down the path to where the gravestone of Alan Foxton stood. "That was the last time we were all here together. I'll see you later, Jo."

Jo waited for her to leave, before following her a few moments later. She had parked her car on the road outside the church. Most of the mourners seemed to be heading back to Hartwell Hall where the wake was taking place. Personally, Jo thought entertaining a bunch of Rupert's relatives was the last thing Lucy needed. She had been through enough in even the fairly short time Jo had known her. When Rupert had disappeared, she had she been left alone to look after Freddie and the Hartwell estate, whilst all the time blaming herself for Rupert's disappearance. The discovery of his body and the following inquest had put her under further strain.

Then she had discovered Guy Lovell, the local MP and someone she considered a friend, had in fact been secretly stalking her. His obsession had led to him threatening her with a gun at Hartwell Hall until Rob, Jack and Jo had arrived just in time to rescue her. Jo had arrested Guy and now she was focusing all her attention on his case. Surely, securing the conviction of a senior member of parliament would be enough to get her transferred back to London.

She drove out of Hartwell and headed towards Northallerton, but her progress was slow. She drummed her fingers on the steering wheel as the queue of traffic she was stuck in crawled along. It was always the same when the Tour de France was on television. Middle-aged men in Lycra clogged up the narrow country lanes with their bikes, all convinced they were Mark Cavendish. It didn't help that the queue was headed by a rumbling tractor.

"No chance of being involved in a high-speed chase around here," she muttered to herself, taking a drag on the cigarette in her right hand and blowing the smoke through the open window. Finally, almost an hour later, she arrived at North Yorkshire's police headquarters.

"The chief constable wants to see you," called out the uniformed sergeant behind the reception desk as soon as he saw her. Jo nodded and hurried up the stairs and down corridor. It must be about the investigation into Guy Lovell. She only hoped it was good news. She knocked loudly on the chief constable's door.

"Come in," called out a deep voice in a broad Yorkshire accent. Jo stepped inside.

"Good morning, sir," she began. The chief constable looked up and smiled. He was a large man with thick grey hair and glasses, who looked more like a kindly grandfather than a senior police officer.

"Ah Sergeant Ormond. I have news about the Lovell case," he said tapping the file on the desk in front of him. "The psychiatric reports have come back, and it seems unlikely that Guy Lovell will be declared fit to stand trial."

Jo stood and stared at him.

"So, he's going to be allowed to get away with what he did, sir?" she asked incredulously.

"Not at all, Sergeant. There can still be a trial, but without the defendant being called to give evidence. We still need to provide the prosecution with as much information as possible. Which brings me to my second bit of news. The magistrates have agreed to grant a search warrant for the Grange." He beamed. *It's about time*, thought Jo. The warrant had been subject to delay after delay.

She suspected pressure had come from Guy's political friends who were keen to avoid bad publicity. One of the Home Secretary's special advisers had made several visits to Northallerton since Guy's arrest. In his official car and his pinstriped suit, he'd insisted he was only there to offer assistance, but Jo didn't trust him. However, all she said to the chief constable was: "Thank you, sir. I'll get on with it straight away."

She left the chief constable's office and had to stop herself from slamming the door behind her. The case against Guy looked as if it was going to be buried in legal procedure, along with her hopes of returning to London. Another thought suddenly occurred to her, and she groaned out loud. How on earth was she going to explain this to Lucy? She gave her head a shake. There was still a chance she might be able to get justice for her friend, and now they had finally been granted a warrant to search Guy's house, she didn't want to waste a second. She went down to the canteen and dragged her deputy, Detective Constable Dawson, away from his tea and crumpets and requested some support from uniform, before heading back to the car park.

HARTWELL GRANGE WAS an imposing, elegant Georgian house, built of mellow York stone, on the edge of the village. There was a columned porch over the front door and shuttered sash windows surrounded by twisted boughs of wisteria. Despite being granted a warrant, nobody on Guy's team had handed over any keys. After a quick recce, Jo decided the back door was the weakest point of entry.

"Come on, put your back into it, Dawson," she ordered, cheerfully grinding the butt of her cigarette beneath her toe as her bulky constable threw himself against the back door for the third time. After more huffing and panting he finally splintered it out of the frame on the fifth attempt.

Jo sent her colleagues to search the reception rooms and

Guy's bedroom, while she headed straight to his office. The place appeared to be exactly as Guy had left it. The calendar hadn't been turned over; there was a pile of stamped, addressed, but unposted envelopes and an empty coffee cup.

Jo pulled on her gloves and paced around the room, pausing to open desk drawers and flick through the filing cabinet, although most of the folders she found were empty. She did discover several bank statements and household bills, but other than an old Christmas card "from Rupert, Lucy and Freddie", there was nothing to link the MP to her friend.

Several Victorian sporting prints lined the wall. She nudged the side of each one and smiled. Behind the one of a spaniel with a pheasant in its mouth was a safe built into the wall, but trying to get the combination from Guy's lawyer would take forever. Jo put her hands on her hips and surveyed the room. She'd only met Guy a few times, but he'd never struck her as someone with much imagination. She went to the desk and yanked open the top right-hand-side drawer. She dropped to her knees and peered up at the underside. There it was. Taped to the bare wood. Not only the combination of the safe, but a list of various passwords for his laptop and email accounts.

Jo tutted to herself. To think he had been trusted with matters of national security. She went over to the safe and entered the combination. The door swung open and she peered inside. There was a stash of photographs, some black and white, some in colour, but all of Lucy. Jo began to flick through, then stopped abruptly when she came to last three images.

They were grainy and in black and white, but they quite clearly showed Lucy and her husband, Rupert. They were on the building site next to the village hall that was now the Hayloft, the property Rob Harrison had converted. In the first, from their expressions and the way Rupert was pointing at Lucy, it looked as though they were arguing. The next one showed Lucy holding a spade while Rupert's face was sneering, and in the final image the spade was raised above her head and there was no sign of Rupert.

Jo groaned out loud. Lucy and Rachel had told her what had happened that night. How Lucy had hit Rupert in self-defence before running away. Rachel had returned to check on him and, finding him gone, got rid of the spade her best friend had used. The two of them had kept what happened a secret. Telling only Jo and their other friend Meera. What Jo hadn't known until now, was that Guy had been there too. His obsession with Lucy must have been consuming him even all those months ago. More importantly, he'd seen what had happened between Lucy and Rupert and he had evidence.

Jo carefully placed most of the photos into evidence bags but kept the ones of Lucy with Rupert separate and slipped them into her pocket. Then without much hope they would have found anything else, she returned to her colleagues.

Several hours later, her prediction had been proved correct. Even though they had searched every inch of the house, they hadn't been able to find anything except the photos, not even the receipt for the camera Guy had planted in Lucy's room. Despite the place looking untouched, her instincts told Jo someone might have been there before them. Guy was a prominent backbench MP and served on the defence committee. She was sure Special Branch or the interfering government adviser would have done a sweep of his house before she and her team had been given permission to enter. It would certainly explain the empty files. Feeling dejected she dismissed the others and drove home.

Her car rumbled to a halt on the cobbles outside the cottage she was renting from the Hartwell estate. The place was in darkness. Meera, her neighbour, was away on holiday in Scotland. She was the village doctor and had arrived in Hartwell with her son, Krish, at the same time as Jo. She was surprised at how much she missed having them around.

Jo had been abandoned when she was only a few hours old and had grown up in a series of children's homes. She'd been shuffled around the capital and kicked out of almost every school she'd attended and never really had anyone she'd been attached to. Boyfriends had drifted in and out of her life and were lucky to last more than a couple of weeks. A police psychologist had once told her she had commitment issues and that she employed a defence mechanism when it came to forming relationships. Jo didn't disagree, but really couldn't see why this was a problem. Keeping people at arm's length and not getting sucked into their dramas had served her well. She was relieved she didn't need anyone. Then she'd moved to Hartwell.

Despite her best efforts, she'd managed to make friends for the first time in her life. Lucy, Meera and Rachel had included her, made her feel welcome and dragged her into their lives. As well as arresting Guy, she had helped Lucy and Rachel get through the inquest into Rupert's death. She'd even helped Rachel when Max had tried to get rid of Bailey, her beloved pony.

Jo put the key into her front door and sighed. Meera and Krish had only been away for ten days, but it felt longer. She missed Meera leaving the food parcels on her doorstep when she'd worked a late shift, she missed popping next door for a cup of tea and a chat, and she missed Krish appearing over the garden fence to show her the latest trick he'd taught Darwin, his ferret, or to raid her stash of crisps and chocolate.

She entered her cottage and flicked on the lights. It was eerily quiet until her stomach rumbled loudly. She went through to the kitchen, yanked open the door of her freezer and peered inside. There was one remaining Tupperware container. The neatly written label informed her it held chicken Balti. Meera was the only doctor Jo had ever met who had legible handwriting. Ignoring her neighbour's precise instructions Jo bunged the container in the microwave, programmed it for five minutes and grabbed a beer from the fridge while she waited. It pinged and she carefully carried the piping-hot container through to the sitting room. Balancing it on her knee, she flicked on the TV and began to eat while she tried to work out what to do about the case against Guy.

THE NEXT MORNING, she woke up in the same place, having fallen asleep on the sofa. The empty plastic carton lay on the floor beside her. She stretched and had a shower, before beginning the day as she always did, with a jog around the village. She wanted to clear her head, before she went to speak to Lucy about what she'd found out the previous day. However, she wasn't alone for long. Soon she heard the heavy footsteps of Jack lumbering up behind her.

"Morning, lovely," he panted as he appeared next to her. Baxter, his black Labrador puppy, was lolloping along by his side. Jo slowed her pace a little. Jack had once been a professional rugby player, but an injury had ended his career and left him with a permanent limp. His face also bore the scars of many scrums and tackles.

"You're out earlier than usual," he commented.

"I've got a lot on my mind," replied Jo.

"I expect you're trying to decide when you're going to let me take you out on another date. Will it be tonight or tomorrow or both?"

Since she'd arrived in the village, Jack had been waging a campaign to convince her to go out with him. So far, they'd had one date. Jack had taken her out to dinner in Harrogate and they'd ended up in a club, where Jo was surprised to discover that Jack was actually a pretty good dancer. Admittedly it had been fun, but she wasn't interested in a relationship. Jo smiled but shook her head.

"No. It's work. We finally searched Guy's house yesterday and I need to go and speak to Lucy about something we found there, but I don't like the idea of bothering her so soon after the funeral."

They had arrived at the glade of trees that surrounded the ancient well that gave the village its name. Jo stopped in the shade and took a sip from her water bottle. Jack sank to his knees, trying to catch his breath as Baxter enthusiastically licked the sweat from his face.

"I think you might be worrying about nothing," puffed Jack. "I know everyone thinks Lucy is this fluffy airhead, but I think she's tougher than she looks."

"I hope you're right." Jo sighed as she stretched her quads. "Come on, I'll race you back to the pub and you can make me a bacon sandwich."

After breakfast and another shower, Jo drove through the ornate black wrought-iron gates and down the sweeping gravel drive that led to Hartwell Hall. The huge building looked imposing as you approached it, but it was only on closer inspection that you noticed the crumbling stonework and flaking paintwork. Lucy was forever trying to come up with schemes to pay for the never-ending maintenance work.

Jo found her on her hands and knees, pulling out weeds that were growing between the crack in the steps that led up to the grand portico entrance.

"Do you want a hand?" she asked, crouching down next to her and tugging at a large clump of grass. Lucy looked up in surprise.

"Oh hi, Jo! Yes, thanks. I've got our first wedding this weekend. It's being held in a marquee on the south lawn, but the bride asked for photos to be taken here, so I want it to look its best. I've wrecked my nails in the process though. I should have bought some gardening gloves."

She was dressed in jeans and an old T-shirt. Her blonde hair was shoved under a baseball cap. Jo glanced at her friend's hands. They were indeed filthy with the chipped remains of a French manicure, yet even in this state Lucy still managed to look effortlessly beautiful and elegant. Jo thought there were women who could spend all day in a salon and a small fortune on couture, and not look as good as her slightly chaotic friend.

"Are you okay after the funeral?" she asked.

Lucy shrugged. "It probably sounds heartless, but I'm simply relieved it's all over," she replied quietly.

They continued to weed in silence for a few minutes, until Lucy spoke again. "This isn't a social call, is it?"

"I'm afraid not."

Lucy rocked back on her heels and sighed. "Let's go inside and I'll put the kettle on. Bad news is always better with a cup of tea."

Brushing the soil off their hands, they walked around to the back of the house where Jo had to negotiate her way past Lucy's three excitable dogs before she could sit down in one of the old armchairs next to the huge Aga. Lucy rushed around, filling the kettle, throwing biscuits to the still-woofing dogs and rummaging through the steaming dishwasher for a clean teaspoon. Finally, when she'd handed a mug of strong tea to Jo, she flopped down in the chair opposite her.

"Okay, what is it? Has the coroner changed his mind?"

"No, it's not about Rupert, at least not directly. It's about Guy."

Lucy turned very pale. "What about him? He's not coming back here, is he?"

"No, no," Jo quickly reassured her. "He's still being assessed in hospital, but it's likely that he'll be declared unfit to stand trial."

Lucy's face creased in confusion. "So, there won't be a trial?"

"There will, but he won't be there and if he is found guilty, he won't be sent to prison."

Lucy began to shake her head slowly. "He'll get away with it. Spying on me, scaring me, threatening me. He won't be punished."

"On the plus side, you won't have to give evidence in front of him," said Jo, trying to find something positive to tell her friend. Lucy nodded silently. "There's something else," continued Jo. "We were finally given a warrant to search his house. I found quite a lot of photos of you."

Lucy's hand flew to her mouth. "Oh God, oh God," she murmured.

Jo wished Rachel or Meera were there too. They were both much better at this kind of thing. Even after all her training about breaking bad news, it still didn't come naturally to her. Awkwardly, she patted Lucy on the arm before continuing cautiously.

"I'm handing most of the stuff we found over to the Crown Prosecution Service, but I found these as well."

She took the photos taken on the night Rupert disappeared and pushed them across the table. Lucy stared down at them for a moment and then looked up at Jo.

"He was there that night. He saw what happened, but he never said anything. Why?"

"It's only my guess, but I think he was going to use them against you. Maybe blackmail you into being with him. Who knows, he's a pretty screwed-up bloke."

"Do you think he could have been involved in Rupert's

death?"

"I don't know," replied Jo. "That was one theory I was working on, but I haven't been able to question him and now I doubt I ever will."

"What are you going to do with these?" asked Lucy gesturing to the photos that she still hadn't touched.

"I'm giving them to you. Officially, we are no longer investigating Rupert's death. These were taken on public land, not a private setting and…" she paused "…I know you didn't kill him. The other photos we found should be enough for the CPS to build the case against Guy."

"Thanks, Jo," whispered Lucy. She seemed lost in her thoughts, chewing her lip nervously, before she spoke again. "There's something else. I wasn't sure whether I should mention it or not, but I can't find Rupert's passport."

"Are you sure?"

"I think so. When he first disappeared, the police asked me about it, and I remember showing them it was still in the drawer of his office desk. Anyway, this morning I was collecting things like the death certificate and our marriage certificate to put in the safe, and I couldn't find it anywhere."

"Could someone have taken it?" asked Jo, remembering that the house would have been full of people after the funeral.

Lucy shrugged. "I suppose so, but who would want to?"

Jo shook her head. She'd almost given up trying to make sense of things when it came to the life and death of Rupert Hanley.

"I don't know, but don't worry about it too much. Maybe it'll turn up."

"Maybe," echoed Lucy, slipping the photos into her pocket.

CHAPTER TWO

L UCY WONDERED IF there was a type of dyslexia for numbers. If there was, she definitely had it. Laid out in front of her were a series of spreadsheets that made her head hurt when she looked at them. Sitting on the other side of the large, leather-topped oak desk was Mr Bradbury, whose firm had been the Hanley family's accountants for years. He was a short, balding man who occasionally looked up at her over his half-moon spectacles as he droned on about assets, liabilities, quarterly receipts, business relief and turnover.

She kept smiling and nodding, terrified he was going to ask her something she wouldn't know how to answer. Perhaps she was in shock. The first piece of information Mr Bradbury had imparted was that following Rupert's death, the estate was subject to forty per cent inheritance tax. Even Lucy with her limited grasp of finances knew that was bad. How was she ever going to be able to pay it?

She gazed over the accountant's bowed, threadbare head and out of the window. Fat raindrops were bouncing off the canvas covering the stalls arranged around the war memorial in Thirsk marketplace. Shoppers were hurrying by, their heads down as they dodged the puddles. It had been raining all day. The previous Tuesday, the day of Rupert's funeral, had been filled with glorious sunshine. It had seemed wrong that a funeral should take place on such a perfect day. Lucy always felt they should be held on cold, damp, bleak days to match the mourners' moods. But how many of those gathered around his grave were truly mourning her late husband? Years of drug abuse and violence had alienated everyone, including her.

She sighed softly. Right now, she wished she was back in the kitchen of Hartwell Hall with Freddie and the dogs, sitting next to the Aga and eating the warm scones Joan had been baking before she left for this miserable meeting. It was no good—she had to escape. Mr Bradbury paused to take a sip of tea from his china cup and Lucy took her chance. She scooped up the spreadsheets and shoved them into her handbag as she quickly rose to her feet.

"Thank you so much, Mr Bradbury. You really have been incredibly helpful. Perhaps I could take all this lovely paperwork home and go though it there. I could call you if I have any questions."

"Yes, yes, as you wish, Lady Hanley," stammered the accountant looking slightly bewildered as he too rose to his feet and hurried to open the door for Lucy.

LUCY DASHED THROUGH the rain, leapt into her car and slammed the door shut in relief. She dumped her bag containing the accountant's paperwork on the passenger seat and turned on the ignition. Nothing. She tried again. The engine spluttered and whined and gasped before dying again.

"Oh bugger," groaned Lucy. Like almost everything else she owned, the Discovery was in desperate need of proper maintenance. It had only just scraped through its last MOT. "Come on, Dizzy, you can do this. Third time lucky!" Sending up a silent prayer, she turned the key again and the four-wheel drive finally juddered to life. With a loud whoop of relief Lucy drove away from the crowded marketplace and out through the open countryside back towards Hartwell. She flicked on the radio, but for once the blaring pop music did nothing to lift her mood. The heavy raindrops bashing against the windscreen and the squeak of the wiper blades reminded her of the last time she'd driven home in the pouring rain.

It was the night she'd realised Guy, the local MP and someone she'd considered a close friend, had been stalking her. She shuddered at the memory of driving home, her heart pounding even more loudly than the rain hitting the car. She had stopped at the White Hart, hoping Rachel—her best friend—would help her; but instead they'd argued, and she'd driven home alone only to find Guy waiting for her. Thanks to Jo, Jack and Rob he'd been arrested, but ever since, she'd kept replaying that night and the events leading up to it. Looking back, it was so easy to spot all the mistakes she'd made. She'd been too trusting. She had thought such an outwardly charming man would take care of her when the opposite was true. It had been the same with Rupert when she'd first met him. Would she never learn her lesson? She shook her head as she drove along, still angry with herself.

Since that night, she'd hidden herself away. Staying at home and concentrating on looking after Freddie, the dogs and the Hall. Reluctantly, she'd come out of hiding to attend the inquest and funeral, but the press attention and the gossip swirling around her at both events had sent her scurrying back home. After the funeral, she'd thought she might be able to put it all behind her and move on, then Jo had arrived with the photos she'd found at Guy's. Lucy's chest tightened at the thought of those images. For months she and Rachel had thought their secret was safe, but Guy had known what had happened that night all along. The question that Jo hadn't raised, but that Lucy couldn't get out of her head, was had he told anyone else?

The rain finally began to ease as she arrived back in Hartwell. She turned through the black wrought-iron gates and passed the gatehouse where Joan and Bill the gardener lived and drove down the long drive that led to her home. Hartwell Hall had been in the Hanley family for hundreds of years, and she hoped that she wouldn't be the one to lose it.

She might not have been socialising recently, but she had been busy coming up with ways for the hall and estate to generate income. The traditional revenue that came from farming and renting out property on the estate no longer came anywhere close to maintaining the Hall. So instead, she'd made the old place look as presentable as possible and started hiring it out for weddings. She had also contacted film and television companies who might want to use it as a location. Much to her surprise these new ventures were going well. She had bookings for weddings every Saturday for the next three months. Most of the couples wanted to hold their reception in a marquee in the grounds, but some asked to hire out the Hall itself for photographs, which was even more lucrative.

Once she'd parked and placed a grateful kiss on Dizzy's bonnet, she headed straight for her office. The room had once been her late father-in-law's dressing room, but she'd removed the wardrobe that smelt of mothballs and the ugly full-length mahogany mirrors and, in their place, installed her desk and computer. Instead of traditional hunting scenes, the walls were now covered in planners, calendars and Post-It notes. Lucy dumped the pile of files from the accountants' on to the desk and stared out of the window. She could see Freddie down by the lake throwing a stick for Root, his new puppy, while Tilly the Labrador and Pickle, the terrier, looked on.

Her son was a quiet, sensible, sensitive little boy. Lucy prayed that everything that had happened with his father and Guy hadn't scarred him too deeply. Recently, he'd been more subdued than usual, but when Lucy had gently enquired if he was okay, he'd simply said he was missing Krish, his best friend who was away on holiday in Scotland. Krish had moved to the village a few months ago and two boys had become firm friends, as had Lucy and his mother, Meera. Lucy smiled to herself. She had some good news about hiring out the Hall and she knew Meera, with her obsession with English literature—particularly Jane Austen and the Brontë sisters—would be more excited than anyone when she heard. A television production company were filming a new adaptation of *Jane Eyre* and wanted to use Hartwell Hall as Thornfield, Mr Rochester's home.

Since the news of a film company possibly wanting to use Hartwell Hall had leaked out, Lucy had to deal with a stream of visitors, who had turned up on the pretence of offering to help. The thought of Hartwell Hall being chosen for a film location had generated much excitement in the village and it was clear some residents had hopes of being discovered themselves. Reverend Davenport had started quoting Shakespeare whenever she saw him, while Becky— Rachel's nightmare of a sister—had been to the tanning salon and nail bar more than usual and her teeth had become suspiciously white. Even Colonel Marsden had begun dropping unsubtle hints about how well received his performance as Ebenezer Scrooge at university had been. So far, Lucy had managed to politely, but firmly, get rid of them all, but heaven knew what they'd be like if filming actually ever started.

Lucy's thoughts were suddenly disturbed when she heard the crunch of tyres on gravel and she turned to see the now familiar sight of the location scout's car heading up the drive. Lucy grabbed her clipboard in a panic. With her head full of accounts, she'd almost forgotten he was coming today. It was an important meeting too. He was bringing the director with him for the final say. If all went well, Lucy would be able to sign the contract today. She glanced back at the files from Mr Bradbury as she headed out the door. They would have to wait. It was more important that she secured income for the estate; hopefully then the accounts would sort themselves out. Fluffing up her hair she hurried downstairs. She ducked into the kitchen and found Joan, her housekeeper, standing next to the Aga.

"Hello, love," said the older woman, looking up from the large bowl of cream she was whipping by hand. "How did the meeting with Mr Bradbury go?"

"Ugh, don't ask!" replied Lucy. "But I've got a bigger problem right now. The film location guy is here with the director. I completely forgot. Any chance you could make us a pot of tea when I've finished showing them around?"

"Don't you worry, love. I remembered you told me about them coming last week. The kettle is already on and I'm preparing the cream and jam to go with the scones I made this morning. I'll bring a tray through into the library as soon as you are ready."

Lucy threw her arms around Joan and hugged her tightly.

"You are an angel. Thank you so much. What would I ever do without you?"

"Now don't be silly," replied Joan who had turned pink. "You go and meet your guests. I'll keep my fingers crossed for you, but I doubt you'll need it. I dare say you'll have them eating out of your hand, but maybe show them the ballroom last. Bill said that patch of mould has appeared again. He painted over it, but it hasn't dried yet."

Joan and her husband Bill lived at the gatehouse at the end of the driveway of Hartwell Hall. Officially they were the housekeeper and gardener, but to Lucy they were more like family. She was certain she wouldn't have managed to get through the last few years without them. Even before Rupert disappeared, life with him had been difficult. He'd spent most of time down in London, but when he did return, he was moody and often violent. Disappearing to see Joan in her cosy little gatehouse or in the kitchen had been Lucy's only sanctuary.

She left the kitchen and headed out through the front door as the people from the film company were stepping out of their car. She might not be any good when it came to accounts, but she was great when it came to dealing with people. She had charm and an ability to put others at ease, whether she was talking to a duke or a delivery driver. After greeting the location scout, the director and his secretary, she gave them a full tour of the hall and gardens. Never having been much of a reader, she'd watched at least three previous adaptations of the novel, so as she showed them around, she could sound knowledgeable and even made a few suggestions of locations in the garden they might want to use as well as the in the hall itself.

Later when they were all sitting in the library enjoying Joan's tea and scones, she managed to remain calm when the contract was handed over to her and not shriek with joy as she signed the deal that would earn the estate thousands of pounds for only a few weeks' disruption.

CHAPTER THREE

M EERA BLINKED AS the early morning light nudged her gently awake. The hand on her brass bedside clock told her the alarm wouldn't be going off for another ten minutes. She snuggled a little deeper under the duvet and stretched out her foot until it made contact with a warm leg, and she smiled to herself. She was slowly getting used to having another person in her bed. They had arrived home late last night after two wonderful weeks in the Scottish Highlands. Ben had been driving for over five hours, so Meera had invited him to stay as she carried a sleeping Krish up to his room. A change in his breathing, followed by the sound of a loud yawn, told her Ben was now awake too. He rolled over and wrapped his arm tightly round her.

"I feel like I've slept for a hundred years," he murmured into her hair. Meera twisted around to face him.

"It's almost six thirty," she whispered.

Ben opened one eye. "Is that your way of telling me I need to get up?"

"It's just that Krish doesn't know you stayed last night."

"He knows we shared a bedroom when we were up in Scotland. He seemed fine about it," replied Ben with another yawn.

"He might feel differently about you staying here though," whispered back Meera.

At that moment, there was a creak on the floorboards outside and quiet voice called out, "Can I come in?"

"Of course, Krish," replied Meera hurriedly sitting up in bed and nudging Ben to do the same. "Come in."

The door slowly opened and Krish walked in, his tongue poking out of the corner of his mouth in concentration as he carried a tray holding two glasses of orange juice and two bowls of cereal.

"I've made you both breakfast in bed," he said proudly. "It's to say thanks for a great holiday."

"What a lovely thought. Thank you, Krish," said Meera pushing her neat black bob away from her face as she propped a pillow behind her. Ben reached out for his glasses on the bedside table.

"This looks great!" he said helping to steady the tray as Krish handed it over. He looked so proud and happy, that Meera didn't care that most of her juice had ended up in her cereal bowl and was now curdling the milk. She didn't even mind when Darwin, the pet ferret Ben had bought for her allergy-prone son, came scurrying into the room and leapt up on to the bed to join them.

AFTER THEIR SLIGHTLY haphazard breakfast, both Ben and Meera had to leave for work at their respective practices. Ben was a vet based in Thirsk and Meera had taken over as Hartwell's GP a few months ago. Before heading to the surgery, Meera dropped Krish off at the holiday club the village school ran. She watched as he charged across the playground to tell Rachel all about the red squirrels and otters he's seen up in Scotland. With a smile she waved goodbye to her son and old university friend before taking the short walk down the lane to the low stone building between the cricket pitch and the village hall, which housed the doctor's surgery.

She said hello to the practice nurse and two receptionists, managing to politely bat away all their pointed questions about whether she and Ben had enjoyed their time away. She also ignored Nora who was waiting for a nurse to treat her bunions, when she loudly declared, "In my day, it wasn't right for a married woman to go swanning off on holiday with a man who wasn't her husband."

Meera went to her consulting room and took a moment to look at her patient list for the day. There were a couple of expectant mothers, but the others were all older members of the village with a variety of ongoing ailments.

Medicine might have been more Meera's parents' choice of career rather than hers, but she was a good doctor partly because she was also a good listener. So often patients, particularly the more elderly ones, would make an appointment for a mild or ongoing complaint. They would arrive and chat away about the weather or the harvest, then as they were about to leave, they'd suddenly say something like: 'By the way, Doctor, I found this lump. It might not be anything but...' Over the years she had developed a six sense about these things.

It was her last appointment of the morning, and Colonel

Marsden was sitting opposite her, giving a blow-by-blow account of how he'd persuaded the rest of the parish council to place the new wooden bench by the stream instead of outside the village hall. She smiled and nodded, waiting for him to get to the real point of his visit. The original appointment had been for a regular check-up of his gouty toe—the nurse had been concerned it wasn't improving so she'd asked Meera to take a look. Meera had prescribed some different medication to reduce the inflammation, but that had been dealt with in the first three minutes.

"As I told the others, Doctor," continued the colonel, "the stream is a far superior location. It might be a little awkward for old fogeys like me walking across the cobbles, but young mothers can sit there with their little ones and feed the ducks."

"I'm sure they'll appreciate that, Colonel, and with a little rest and your new medication, walking over the cobbles shouldn't be a problem for you either," said Meera, giving him a reassuring smile.

"I certainly hope so," replied the colonel, rising to his feet, "although—" *here it comes*, thought Meera "—I have been getting the odd dizzy spell of late. Probably nothing to worry about though."

"Perhaps not, but why don't you let me take your blood pressure to be sure. According to your notes, we haven't checked it since Easter," she suggested gently. The colonel sat down again with a quick nod of this head.

"Very well, Doctor. If you think I should."

He removed his jacket, rolled up his sleeve and sat very still, breathing deeply with his back ramrod straight as Meera attached the cuff and tightened it around his arm. She took the reading. It was sky high. One hundred and fifty over ninety.

"I'm afraid you are suffering from hypertension, Colonel. I'll prescribe you some pills that should help, and I would like you to pop in and have the nurse take your blood pressure every week."

"More pills. I'll be rattling at this rate," he grumbled, rolling down his sleeve, but he looked relieved. "But they'll stop the light-headedness, will they? I don't want to suddenly keel over in the middle of the village when I'm walking the dogs."

"They should certainly help, as will gentle exercise," she reassured him. "And perhaps a change in diet. Lowering your salt intake and maybe reducing your units of alcohol."

"I'm already down to only one or two glasses a day because of the gout," protested the colonel. "And I've switched brandy for gin and claret for Chablis. I don't know. Why is it that everything I enjoy is bad for me?" He continued grumbling as he made his way to the door Meera was holding open for him. She smiled sympathetically, but she'd seen the colonel's idea of a unit of alcohol when he was in charge of the bar at the cricket club, and it was about three times the government recommendations.

"I'd like to see you again in a week, Colonel. Will you make an appointment at the reception desk?"

He nodded in response and gave her a brisk wave goodbye with his walking stick. Meera glanced at her watch. She had ten minutes until her first afternoon appointment, so she went through to the small kitchen at the back of the surgery to make herself a cup of her favourite green tea. As the kettle began to boil, she let her mind wander back to Scotland. This time yesterday, she'd been sitting on a tartan blanket by the edge of a loch eating salmon sandwiches from a picnic basket and drinking tea from a flask while Ben taught Krish how to skim stones. It had felt like heaven.

But it wasn't just the location, but being with Ben. For the first time she felt she'd found someone who loved her just as she was. Ben didn't tell her she was being silly and frivolous when she talked about her favourite books. He didn't mind that she had a tendency to worry and overthink things. He always considered her concerns calmly and seriously. Most of all, she adored the way he always put her and her son's happiness first. He had planned the entire holiday around them. From taking Krish over to the Isle of Mull so Krish could see eagles, to taking a huge detour just so she could see Balmoral. It was the sort of life she had always longed for.

She was suddenly distracted by a tapping sound on the window. She turned to see Ben's face grinning back at her. Her heart gave a little skip as she hurried to open the door.

"This is a lovely surprise! What are you doing here?" she asked reaching up to kiss him as he stepped inside.

"I'm on my way up to Dan Foxton's farm to check on a new ram he's bought, but I wanted to call in and see you. I've got something to show you," he said producing a glossy brochure from behind his back with an uncharacteristic flourish. Meera took it from him. There was a photo of an elegant stone manor house standing in the middle of a beautiful garden with a stream running through it.

"The Grange, Hartwell," read Meera, "a distinguished Georgian house, privately situated in immaculate gardens, with glorious views, on the edge of one of Yorkshire's most well-loved villages."

"It's Guy's house," explained Ben. "It's going on the market at the weekend. I called into the estate agent's office and the brochures had just arrived from the printers. We are going to be the first people to see it before they start advertising and sending copies to people on their mailing list."

"It is exactly how I imagined Longbourn," sighed Meera as she flipped through the pages.

Ben frowned for a second. "*Sense and Sensibility?*"

"*Pride and Prejudice,*" replied Meera with a smile as she paused to admire the polished wooden staircase that rose from the reception hall, turning several times before leading you to the galleried landing.

"Why did the agent give you a copy? And what do you mean we are going to be the first people to see it?"

"I told him that I was looking for family home near Hartwell, or rather we are."

"Are we?" asked Meera, looking up in surprise. It was true while they were staying at the lovely holiday home in Scotland with its turrets and views of the mountains and lochs, she'd daydreamed aloud about how wonderful it would be if they could stay there together forever. As they'd sat sipping whisky late at night, after Krish had gone to bed, they had each described their perfect house and joked about how wonderful it would be to find it in Hartwell, but she didn't feel they'd discussed it properly. Ben adjusted his glasses and looked a little confused.

"Aren't we? It seemed like the next natural step to me. Finding a family home for the three of us, four including Darwin, although he doesn't take up much space. You've made your cottage look lovely, but I am in serious danger of knocking myself out on these low beams one day."

It was true. Standing at over six foot three, Ben really wasn't built for living in her cottage.

"What about your flat in Thirsk?" she asked.

"It was only ever meant to be a stopgap. I only chose it because it's so close to the surgery. I always hoped to meet the right person, get married and find a proper family home one day."

Meera stared at him for a second. He had a way of making everything sound so simple, but her life was far from that.

"It sounds lovely, except I'm already married," she said, quietly. She'd let herself be swept along with the idea of them all living together, but realistically how could she when she was still married to Dev? Moving away from Bradford had been one thing but moving into a house with another man was quite another. Her parents had grudgingly accepted her move to Hartwell, and they knew all wasn't well with Dev, but she hadn't even told them she'd been on holiday with Ben. How shocked they would be if she suddenly announced she was moving in with another man. Then she would have to deal with all the subsequent questions about Dev. She would have to share secrets that weren't hers to tell. Another thought suddenly occurred to her.

"What about Lucy? How will she feel about us living in Guy's house?"

"Let's just view the place. You might hate it," said Ben as reasonable and level-headed as ever. Meera looked back down at the brochure in her hand and sighed. She knew she wouldn't hate it. She'd already fallen in love with the place.

THAT EVENING, MEERA carefully lit the citronella candles she had stocked up on in Scotland and placed them on the table in the garden while Krish carried an extra chair out for her. She had invited Lucy, Rachel and Jo around for supper. Ben was spending the night at his flat as he was on call and, although she missed him, she was looking forward to catching up with her friends.

It was a warm evening, so she had decided to cook salmon with a parsley and dill sauce. She'd made it with the herbs her mother had helped her plant in the garden. She grabbed a handful of mint for the potatoes too and breathed in the scent. It immediately transported her back to the little house in Bradford where they'd lived when they first moved to England. The back garden was tiny and had been mostly paved over, but her mother had lined up terracotta pots outside the door and filled each one with her favourite herbs. It had been one of Meera's jobs to go and pick whatever she needed.

Helping her mother cook had ignited Meera's passion for food. She loved cooking, especially for others. However, for a long time it had been only her and Krish, whose dishes of choice were either fish fingers or pizza. She had stopped inviting her family over when avoiding the inevitable questions about Dev's whereabouts became too difficult. Since moving to Hartwell, finding Rachel again and meeting Lucy and Jo, she'd relished the chance to entertain them in her little cottage.

Jo was the first to arrive. She had brought some beer with her and a large box of sweets that she quickly passed to Krish, who promptly dashed upstairs, while Meera pretended not to notice. She led Jo out to the garden and directed her to the seat opposite her own.

"I thought you could sit there, then Rachel and Lucy won't have to sit next to each other, you know in case things are still awkward between them."

For years Rachel had harboured a crush on her best friend, which everyone seemed to know about except Lucy herself. She had finally found out on the night Guy was arrested. Jo popped the top off one of the beers and sat down.

"Okay, but they seem fine to me. Although, to be honest I've hardly seen Lucy. She's being keeping a very low profile. Not that I blame her. The place was crawling with press for a while."

Meera picked up the bottle Jo was drinking from and carefully poured the beer into a tall glass instead.

"How was the funeral?" she asked. "How were Lucy and Freddie? I felt bad I missed it and wrote and told her how sorry I was."

"You didn't miss much. Lots of people wearing black and trying to look sad, while the Rev droned on. Lucy said she's relieved it's all over. I did feel sorry for Freddie though. It must be tough losing your dad when you are so young."

Meera nodded sympathetically. "Lucy's bringing him tonight, so hopefully seeing Krish again will cheer him up a bit. Is there any news about Guy?"

Jo pulled a face. "It looks like he'll be declared unfit to stand trial."

Meera frowned. She worried about Lucy a lot. Although she might seem carefree to others, Meera had seen her medical records and knew what she had been through during the last few years of her marriage to Rupert. Then with Guy terrifying her like that, it was incredible how she had managed to hold everything together.

"What does that mean? Won't he be punished for what he did? How does Lucy feel about this?"

"Yes, I told her. She seemed okay."

Before Jo could say any more, an excited shout from Krish told them that Lucy and Freddie had arrived with Rachel not far behind. Meera bustled around her friends, pouring drinks and bringing out the bowls of salad, crusty bread and minted new potatoes.

"Thank you for running the holiday club today. Krish said he really enjoyed it," she told Rachel, who smiled back at her.

"I'm pleased. He certainly kept us all entertained with his holiday stories."

"Did he?" she asked in surprise. Like Freddie, Krish had a tendency to be quiet around other children, which probably explained why the two of them got along so well. "I don't think I've ever seen him as happy as when he spotted his first red squirrel in the wild."

"And what about you, Meera?" asked Lucy. "Did you

have wonderful time with Ben? People often say a holiday can make or break a relationship."

"It certainly didn't break us. It was heaven." Meera laughed happily, then she paused, not sure if this was the right time, but Lucy seemed quite relaxed despite what Jo had said about Guy's trial. "Actually, there was something I wanted to ask you about, Lucy."

"Me?" asked Lucy, looking surprised. Meera went into the kitchen and returned with the sales particulars for the Grange.

"Ben and I have been talking about buying a house together and, well, Guy's house is about to come on the market," she said, her words tumbling out in a rush.

"Crikey, Meera! That's quick work!" exclaimed Rachel.

Meera smiled shyly. "I know, I know, and it might not come to anything, and I am still married to Dev, and heaven knows what I'll tell my parents. It's all a mess, but it's a lovely house and Ben seemed so proud he'd got the brochure before anyone else." She paused, knowing she sounded nervous and turned her attention back to Lucy. "But I did want to make sure you wouldn't mind. If you think it would be strange me living there, in what was Guy's home, I won't go and look. We can always wait for something else to become available."

Lucy smiled across at her and shook her head firmly.

"I'm happy just knowing that this means he won't be coming back to the village. You are right. It is a lovely house and it would make a wonderful home for you and Ben and Krish. I'll keep my fingers crossed that the viewing goes well. The gardens are beautiful too."

"They are, aren't they," agreed Meera with relief, then glancing around the table, said, "And what do you all think? About the idea of Ben and me moving in together. Is it really too soon, do you think?"

"It doesn't matter what we think, it's how you feel, Meera," said Rachel reasonably.

"But that's just it." Meera sighed. "I've fallen in love with Ben and as soon as I saw the Grange I fell in love with that too, but the sensible side of my brain keeps telling me we've only known each other a few months."

Rachel groaned. "You were just like this at university. You'd suddenly decide to be brave and announce you would come to a party with us all or even go on holiday, then almost immediately you would start worrying and end up backing out. Yes, in an ideal world it might be easier to explain to your family if you and Dev got divorced first, but the world isn't ideal and if Dev doesn't want a divorce, you could be waiting for years. Sometimes, you need to take a risk, even if it doesn't work out."

"I suppose you might be right," said Meera quietly. Her oldest friend's words had stung a little.

"Oh," said Lucy suddenly, "I remember reading your horoscope this morning—it was a good one. Let me think now." She screwed up her face as she tried to remember. "Yes, that's it. *Pisces, be bold with the decisions you make today. The outlook is sunny.*"

"Oh, that does sound positive," replied Meera, brightening.

Jo rolled her eyes. "Seriously? You're a doctor, Meera. How can you believe in that rubbish? But, for what it's worth, I think you should go for it. Of course, if it was up to me, Ben would move in here. That way I still keep you as a neighbour and if you go off him, you can just kick him out."

"Jo!" exclaimed Rachel, then turning to Lucy, asked, "What did today's horoscope say for Virgo? *Stop being such a selfish, cynical pessimist or your friends will all stop speaking to you?*"

"Ha, ha," said Jo good-naturedly. "I'm not a pessimist, I'm a realist." She picked up the brochure for the Grange and began leafing through. "You should get it for a good price. I bet Guy wants a quick sale. He will probably need the cash for his defence. Those lawyers of his must cost a fortune, but I guess he must think it's worth it if he gets out of going to court. These photos don't do it justice though. It looks better when you see it for real."

"Have you been inside?" asked Meera eagerly. Their viewing wasn't until the weekend, and she couldn't wait to hear more about the place.

Jo nodded. "Yep, we finally got a warrant." She took a sip of beer. "But I should warn you, you might need a new back door. We found plenty of evidence against him though. The creep had kept loads of photos."

Meera cringed as Rachel not very subtly kicked Jo underneath the table.

"Ow! What was that for?" she cried out, rubbing her ankle. "I've already told Lucy what we found."

Meera decided to quickly change the subject. Lucy had grown silent and was fiddling with the stem of her wine glass. She had been very gracious about Meera's interest in the Grange, but she probably didn't want to dwell on the reason it was now available.

"So, Rachel, do you think you'll be able to get away over the summer? Maybe go and join Sarah out in Peru?" she asked as she topped up everyone's glasses. Sarah Stevenson was an archaeologist. She had arrived in the village when an ancient Druid burial ground had been discovered and had invited Rachel out on a date. The two of them had hit it off, but at the beginning of the summer, Sarah had left for a working holiday in South America.

Rachel shrugged. "I'm not sure. We're still waiting to hear back about the tests Mum had while you were away. I don't want to go anywhere until she's been given the all clear, and even if the news is good, I doubt I'll have the time to get to South America and back. I've already promised I'll be here for the village fete. Mum and Dad always used to run the tombola together. This will be the first year without him. I can't let her do it on her own."

"Oh my God!" Lucy exclaimed suddenly, her hand flying to her mouth. "The village fete! I'd completely forgotten about it."

"What's the problem?" asked Jo looking puzzled.

"The Hartwell village fete takes place on the last weekend in August every year," Lucy began to explain. "It's always held in the grounds of the Hall, but I've taken a booking for a wedding that weekend. Oh no! Caroline is going to kill me," groaned Lucy. "Only the other day she was going on about how important village traditions are."

The others could only nod sympathetically. Caroline, Lucy's mother-in-law, was not the understanding sort. Although she no longer lived in Hartwell Hall, she still treated the village as if it was her personal property.

"Can't it be held somewhere else?" asked Meera. She had heard lots about this very traditional English village fete from her patients and colleagues at work and had been looking forward to it; so had Krish. Lucy shook her head.

"There isn't really anywhere else big enough," explained Rachel. "We need a large flat area of grass to set the stalls up on. There aren't any other gardens in the village big enough."

"What about the cricket ground?" suggested Jo.

"You must be joking," snorted Rachel as Lucy grimaced.

"I don't know what would be worse, trying to convince Colonel Marsden and the rest of the club to let us ruin their pitch or tell Caroline I've messed up again," she groaned.

Meera patted her sympathetically on the shoulder. "Never mind. Don't worry about it now. We might be able to come up with something. The important thing is that the Hall is making money."

"That reminds me," said Lucy her face suddenly lighting up. "Guess where the new version of *Jane Eyre* is going to be filmed?"

"No!" squealed Meera in excitement. "Oh my goodness, Lucy, that is exciting. Wait until I get the salmon. I want to hear all about it."

They spent the rest of the evening discussing the upcoming shoot. Each coming up with a wish list of actors they hoped might turn up in the Hartwell. As it began to grow dark, Lucy was the first to stand up to leave.

"I hate to break up the party, but I should get Freddie home and I have a meeting with another prospective bride first thing," she apologised.

"I should go too," said Jo knocking back the rest of her beer. Meera showed them out and told Krish to get ready for bed.

As the others left, Rachel hung back and when Meera returned to the garden, Rachel's face looked even more serious than usual.

"Can I have a quiet word?" she asked.

"Of course," replied Meera, wondering if she wanted to talk about her mother who had been experiencing worrying bouts of forgetfulness. "Is it about Mary? Has something happened?"

"No, she's actually been okay recently, but something a bit odd happened when you were away. It was my turn to run the holiday club again last Wednesday and during morning playtime I was looking after a little girl in year two who had fallen over and scraped her knee. One of the older boys came running over to tell me there was a strange man at the gate. I ran over there straight away, but he'd gone by the time I got there. The thing is when I questioned the boy about him, it sounded like he was asking about Krish."

Meera stared at her friend as panic swept through her.

"Are you sure? Who was it? Could it have been Nish? He and my parents didn't know I was away," asked Meera, wondering if her brother would come looking for them, hoping there might be an innocent explanation, but Rachel shook her head.

"No, I asked the children who had seen him to describe him, and they said he was white with a shaved head and a strange mark on his neck. I thought it could be someone connected to Dev. I know you were worried about him trying to take Krish away when you first moved here. When you talked about moving in with Ben, I wondered if he could have heard something."

Meera felt her throat tighten and her heart began to pound. "As far as I know Dev's still in India. The last time we spoke we didn't discuss divorcing and he isn't aware that Ben and I are together, or at least I don't think he is." She spoke softly as her mind raced through who this strange man could be and what it might mean for her and her son. Rachel reached out and gave her arm a squeeze.

"Try not to worry too much. Maybe it was an old friend trying to track you down. I informed the police and Jo asked around the village, but nobody, not even nosy Nora, had seen anything, and he hasn't been spotted since."

Meera nodded as Rachel hugged her goodbye, but as she closed the door, she couldn't shake the feeling of dread that had taken over. Dev had first threatened to take Krish away and fight her for custody when she'd moved to Hartwell. Ben knew how worried she'd been and had arranged for some of Rob's joiners to install more security measures while they were away. Carefully, she slid the new bolts across the front door and went through into the kitchen. She had thought of sitting in the garden, reading a chapter of her book, but now she firmly closed and locked the back door too, feeling like a prisoner in her own home.

She resisted the urge to phone Ben and tell him what Rachel had said. It wasn't fair to worry him when he was working. Since seeing him earlier in the day, she'd done nothing but think about the Grange and how wonderful it would be to live there with him, but now she didn't care where she and Krish lived as long as they were safe.

Chapter Four

R ACHEL WATCHED WITH unblinking eyes as the second hand on the wall clock ticked another minute away. Why did time always pass so slowly in these places? Mary, her mother, was sitting on the blue plastic chair next to her. She was reading an old copy of *Woman's Realm* or at least pretending to. The waiting room was full of friends and neighbours from the village, people Mary would normally have chatted to happily, but today she had just nodded politely before avoiding all eye contact.

There was a lingering smell of paint in the air from the newly decorated walls. A collection of pot plants covered the table in the middle of the room and classical music played quietly in the background, to help those waiting relax and to provide a little more privacy when patients were speaking to the receptionist. These were only a couple of the improvements Meera had made since taking over the practice. Rachel was relieved it was her old university friend they were seeing today and not Dr Robertson who had finally retired earlier that year. In Rachel's opinion, he should have done so much earlier. He had been next to useless when her father was ill.

Rachel stifled a yawn. She had barely slept last night, thinking about what Meera might tell them today. Over the past few months, Mary had become more and more forgetful. She couldn't remember where she'd put things, or she'd forget to turn the oven off. At first, Rachel had put it down to her still grieving for her husband, but as time passed, she seemed to be getting worse and she was starting to become a danger to herself.

As soon as the summer term had finished, Rachel had left her little cottage opposite the village school and moved back to the family farmhouse, so she could keep an eye on her mother. On the days she was busy with the holiday club, she had organised a rota of Mary's many relatives and friends to pop in and keep her company, including Joan and Shirley, Jack's mum. Much to Rachel's surprise, even the fearsome Caroline had offered to help out. Before Meera had gone on holiday, she had arranged for Mary to have various tests and brain scans to find any signs of dementia. Today they would receive the results.

Somewhere down the corridor a door opened. There was the sound of quick, light footsteps and a few seconds later, Meera appeared. She called out Mary's name and gave them both an encouraging smile before leading them back to her consulting room.

"I hope it's good news. I was only thinking this morning, I haven't had any accidents or mishaps since Rachel moved in with me. In fact, I was feeling a bit silly for bothering you at all, Meera."

Rachel put her hand on Mary's arm to quieten her. She always chattered on like this when she was really nervous.

"Why don't you sit down and let Meera tell us the results, Mum. Good or bad," she said gently.

"It is good news," said Meera quickly. "Both the brain scans came back clear. As for all the other tests—" she motioned to the file in front of her "the final results arrived an hour ago. There is no indication you are suffering from dementia or any other disease, Mary."

Rachel stared at her friend's calm serious face for a second as the feeling of relief crashed over her like a wave. Suddenly Mary grabbed her hand and burst into noisy tears. Rachel immediately threw her arm around her and pulled her close.

"It's okay, Mum. You're fine."

"I'm sorry, Meera. I'm just so relieved," sobbed Mary apologetically.

Meera hurriedly passed over the box of tissues that were sitting on her desk and made lots of reassuring noises as Rachel comforted her mother until her tears subsided and she began wiping her eyes.

"But what about all the things that happened?" asked Rachel. "There must be some explanation."

Meera shook her head. "It is puzzling, but all I can tell you is that there is no physical explanation for the lapses in memory. I have wondered if the problem might be psychological. Mary, you have mentioned the shock of losing your husband and the anguish you felt about not being with him when he died."

Mary nodded as the tears began to fall again. Meera quickly passed a handful of leaflets over to Rachel.

"This might not be the right time, but I found some names of grief counsellors and therapists who Mary may like to speak with."

"That's probably a good idea," replied Rachel, who was struggling not to break down in tears of relief herself. "I'll take them home with us if that's okay."

"Of course. I understand. Come back and see me whenever you are ready."

Meera ushered them out of her consulting room and Rachel hurried her mother out through the waiting room. Gasps and murmurs followed them as the other patients saw Mary's damp, red, blotchy face.

BACK AT THE farmhouse, Rachel rolled her shoulders forward and back, and massaged her neck as she waited for the kettle to boil. She hadn't realised how tense she'd been until Meera delivered her news.

"Why don't you follow your new friend out to South America, now that we know I'm not going doolally," suggested Mary who was fussing over Jenny, their old Border collie. She had gone upstairs for half an hour after they'd come back from seeing Meera and when she'd returned to the kitchen had declared she felt much better. Rachel shook her head as she made them both a cup of tea. It was wonderful that the tests and scans had been negative, but she felt Meera had presented them with more questions than answers. As tempting as it might be to join Sarah in Peru, she couldn't disappear to the other side of the world while they hadn't got to the bottom of what was causing Mary's problems.

"No, Mum. It's too late. She's already been out there for

three weeks and besides I don't want to leave you here alone while Becky is away too."

True to form, her selfish sister and hopeless husband had decided to take Araminta, their little girl, to Florida after the funeral instead of waiting to hear about Mary. They were quite happy to use her mother as some sort of personal cash machine, but didn't care enough to see what the outcome of today's appointment was.

"At least go out for a drink tonight. You and Lucy always used to go to the quiz together. You haven't been for weeks. Meera told you I'm not ill. You've been very good to look after me, but you can stop fussing now. Go and have some fun."

Rachel eventually gave in and called Jo, Meera and Lucy to see if they wanted to join her. Lucy made an excuse of having masses of paperwork to sort out. Rachel wasn't entirely surprised as she'd barely been seen in the village recently, but the other two agreed to meet her at the pub for the quiz. She was particularly pleased Meera was happy to leave Krish with Ben. Since Rachel had told her about the strange man at the school, she'd been pretty uptight. The three of them sat at what Rachel thought of as 'their table' in the window.

"Are you going to try and get away for a few days now you know your mum is okay?" asked Jo.

Rachel shrugged. "Mum said I should, but I don't know." She sighed. "Even though the tests didn't find anything, all those things still happened. The oven being left on, stuff disappearing. I don't like the idea of leaving her alone, until we find out what was going on."

"Couldn't Becky keep an eye on things for a week or so?" asked Meera. "It doesn't seem fair that you have to do everything for your mum when she has another daughter living in the village too."

Rachel rolled her eyes at the mention of her sister. "Becky always likes to remind me that, unlike me, she has a child to take care of. Besides, right now, she and Max are out in Florida. They've taken Araminta to Disney World. From the look of all the photos they've been emailing back to Mum, they're having a great time. So great they haven't even bothered to phone to ask about the results."

Jo, who had been fiddling with her beer mat, cleared her throat. "Look," she began, "I wouldn't normally suggest this and I wouldn't say anything in front of Lucy after what happened, but seeing as she isn't here... Maybe you could set up a camera in the farmhouse. That way you could keep an eye on your mum, even if you went abroad."

"You want me to spy on my mum?!" asked Rachel, horrified at the thought.

Jo sighed. "You don't have to think of it as spying. Loads of people have cameras in their homes. Admittedly, some are there to keep an eye on nannies or cleaners if they think they are up to something dodgy, but other people just like to see what their pets do while they're out all day."

"That's true," agreed Meera. "One of my colleagues back in Bradford had a diabetic cat she adored, and she kept an eye on her with a camera she'd installed in the kitchen. In the city, a lot of people have them at their front door for security."

"Exactly. Security," added Jo. "Let's face it, how well do

you really know the guys who work on the farm?"

Rachel looked at her incredulously.

"Tony and Mick? They've worked for us for ages. They think the world of Mum," protested Rachel.

"Did you give them a proper background check before you employed them?"

Rachel shook her head. She'd never met anyone as suspicious as Jo. "I don't know. It wouldn't feel right."

"It might be worth considering, Rachel," said Meera, gently. "Not that I think someone is trying to harm your mum, but as you said yourself, something has clearly been going on. I've been trying to think what the cause could be, since all the tests came back negative. I've been doing some research and I was wondering if your mother had any history of sleepwalking?"

Rachel screwed up her face.

"Not that I know of. Why?"

"Well, she's had a stressful time with your dad passing away and the whole lockdown situation. Sometimes stress can lead to sleepwalking. People have been recorded doing all sorts of strange things while still fast asleep, even cooking a full meal, and your mum did mention that some of the incidents had occurred while she'd been napping or during the night."

"That is true." Rachel nodded. "But I don't know. It would feel sneaky setting up a camera without telling Mum."

"It might be better if she didn't know," reasoned Meera. "Subconsciously it may make her change her behaviour."

"I don't mind setting up for you," added Jo.

At that moment, Jack appeared from behind the bar

wearing his gold sequined jacket to announce the quiz was about to start.

Rachel took a quick sip of her drink. "Okay. Let's do it," she agreed.

THEY DIDN'T DO as well as usual in the quiz that night. Rachel had the feeling all three of them were distracted. Jo was still miffed about the Guy case, while Meera's head was full of thoughts about the Grange and the mystery man at the school. Rachel for her part couldn't stop thinking that thanks to Jo's suggestion, she might finally be able to escape, even if it was only for a week or so. She needed to get away, to have time to think. The last year had been so stressful— losing Dad, not knowing what was going on with Mum and the whole messy, mixed-up business with Lucy and Rupert. She needed to re-evaluate. Decide what she wanted to do with her life.

When she returned to the farmhouse, she found that Mary had already gone to bed. Rachel let Jenny out for a last run, while she made herself a cup of tea and settled on the sofa in the living room and opened her laptop. She began searching for last-minute holiday deals, focusing on Spain, Italy and France, not wanting to go too far away. She wanted somewhere interesting, not simply to sit on a beach for a week with a load of other Brits turning pink in the sun, as they desperately tried to get a tan before heading home. Scrolling past package deal after package deal to Benidorm and Alicante, she suddenly stopped. A week in Italy, flights from Manchester to Naples, with an organised trip to see Pompei and Vesuvius included.

It was perfect. Her finger hovered over the mouse. The flashing sign said there were only two places left. The flight left on the day Becky and Max were due to return from America, but it was no good. Before she could book, she felt she had to let her sister know. Camera or no camera, she would feel better leaving if she knew Becky would at least be checking in on Mary. She quickly fired off an email to her sister telling her Mary had been give the all-clear and that she was thinking of booking a holiday. To her surprise, only a couple of minutes later, she received a reply.

Great news! Go for it! You deserve a break. We'll keep an eye on Mum x

Rachel shook her head. Wonders would never cease! Becky actually thinking of someone else for once. She immediately clicked on the deal and entered her credit card details. It was booked! A few days from now, she'd be roaming the streets of Napoli! She closed her laptop with a sense of achievement as Jenny came plodding back into the room. The old sheepdog settled down next to her with heavy sigh and rested her head on Rachel's knee. She looked up at with slightly cloudy eyes. Rachel stroked her soft, silky ears.

"If only you could talk, old girl," she murmured. "I bet you could tell me what's been going on and we wouldn't need Becky or these cameras, would we?"

Rachel checked her phone again. There was a message from Sarah asking how her mum was. Rachel smiled to herself. It was almost midnight, but in Peru it would be early evening. The two of them may only have been on one date, but that night Sarah had invited her to join her in South

America, partly working on an archaeological dig and partly having the holiday of a lifetime. Rachel would have given anything to join her out there, but as usual life in Hartwell had got in the way. What with the problems with her mother's health and waiting for the outcome of the inquest into Rupert's death, Rachel had had to turn Sarah's offer down, but they had been emailing each other regularly.

Rachel found she looked forward more and more to Sarah's news from Peru and couldn't wait for her to come home. She quickly replied to Sarah, telling her the news about her mum and that she was treating herself to a trip to Italy. She paused before she pressed send and quickly added, *Wish you could join me. Love, Rachel.*

CHAPTER FIVE

B ALANCING PRECARIOUS ON top of a stepladder, with a screwdriver clamped between her teeth, Jo was beginning to regret volunteering to fit the surveillance cameras in Mary's kitchen. Rachel had taken her mother to lunch in York and would be away for about two hours. In theory, this should have given Jo plenty of time, but the instructions were all in Korean and she hadn't bargained for how hard the thick stone farmhouse walls were.

"Do you need a hand?" asked a familiar voice as Jack came strolling in through the back door. Turning around in surprise, Jo dropped the screwdriver and, feeling the steps wobble beneath her feet, she crashed to the floor.

"What are you doing here?" she demanded, ignoring his outstretched hand as she clambered to her feet.

Jack looked at her with concern. "Are you okay? Rachel told me what you were doing, and I thought you might need some help."

"Thanks very much. You startling me like that was exactly what I needed," Jo replied sarcastically, rubbing the bruised hip she'd landed on. "I was managing fine and we were meant to be keeping this camera thing quiet."

"I can be discreet," Jack protested, bending down to

stroke Jenny, who had hobbled from her bed in the corner to greet him enthusiastically. He straightened up and frowned at the camera that was half hanging off the wall. Jo followed his gaze.

"The walls are much harder than I expected," she muttered.

"Couldn't you balance it on top of one of the cupboards or something?" he asked.

"No, it needs to be that high to cover both doors into the room. Once it's in position properly it will blend in with the black wrought-iron curtain pole," explained Jo, through gritted teeth. "I've got it all set up and ready to start recording. It just needs securing."

"Then it's a good thing I came armed," Jack said, pulling a drill out of his back pocket and spinning it on his finger before aiming it at the wall like it was a pistol. Jo smiled despite herself. She hated having to accept help from anyone, but they only had twenty minutes until Rachel and Mary returned. She picked up the stepladder and held it steady for Jack to climb up. A few noisy seconds later, he was back down again.

"All done," he declared triumphantly. "Now are you coming over to the Hart for lunch?"

Jo shook her head. "No thanks, my shift starts in an hour. I'll grab something in Northallerton. Are you okay locking up?" she replied, scooping up her phone and car keys from the kitchen table.

"Don't worry about it. Mary never locks the back door. She's got Jenny to guard the place, hasn't she, old girl," replied Jack cheerfully, bending down to stroke the ageing sheepdog again.

Jo walked out of the farmhouse still shaking her head. Perhaps if the Foxtons were a little more security-conscious there wouldn't have been any need for a camera in the first place. She didn't buy Meera's sleepwalking theory and despite Rachel's confidence in the farm staff, she thought someone was up to no good. Making Mary believe she was confused or absent-minded could be the perfect cover if you wanted to partake in some petty pilfering or worse.

WHEN SHE ARRIVED at the station, she found her office was deserted. Everyone else was out at lunch. Sitting down at her desk, she tore open the sandwich she'd bought from the mini supermarket on her way in. She'd only taken one bite when her phone on the desk began to ring. Gulping down the bread and cheese, she picked up the receiver.

"Ormond," she said, managing not to choke.

"Ah, Sergeant! I'm pleased I got you," said the unmistakably cheerful voice of the duty sergeant from down on the reception desk. "You are just the person I'm looking for, what with your background in narcotics."

"Really?" asked Jo with interest, swinging her legs down from where they had been resting on her neighbour's chair and sitting up a little straighter.

"Yes. The head teacher from Thirsk Grammar has been in touch. There have been reports of someone trying to sell cannabis to students at the school gates. I said you'd call in and have a word. I though it sounded right up your street."

"Thanks, Sarge," replied Jo, her heart sinking. For a second, she thought there might be chance of a decent case. Instead, she now had to drive almost all the way home again and sort out a few kids smoking dope. "Hold on a second," she said as a thought occurred to her. "Isn't it the summer holidays?"

"That's right," agreed the desk sergeant, "but the school is running a holiday club for its students. Trying to keep them out of trouble." He chuckled. "You'd best get a move on. I said you'd be there before they finish at three thirty."

Jo arrived at the school as the final bell was ringing and pushed her way through the throng of noisy students heading out of the main door. Instead of their navy school uniforms most were dressed in sports kit. Heading towards the reception desk, she sniffed the air and shuddered. Why did all schools smell the same? An unmistakable combination of boiled cabbage, disinfectant and sweaty bodies. It took her straight back to her own school days and they certainly didn't hold any happy memories.

The head teacher's secretary ushered her into the office where Ms Mountford was tapping away at her keyboard. A slim, blonde woman in a red trouser suit, she looked much younger than Jo had expected. She sprang to her feet and extended her hand when the secretary introduced Jo.

"Thank you for coming out so quickly, Sergeant."

"No problem, Ms Mountford. I understand you have a complaint about a man selling drugs on school property."

"Yes, although strictly speaking he was outside our boundaries. He was spotted by the gate next to the playing fields; in fact it's the second time this gentleman has been seen there. Fortunately, on this occasion, our PE teacher, Mr Husthwaite, leapt into action and managed to take a photo of him and his car with his mobile. I have the images on my computer. Can I forward them to you? I mean that is all right, isn't it? It's not an invasion of privacy or anything? I want to make sure we are doing everything by the book."

Jo nodded her head. As far as she was concerned someone's right to privacy or anything else ended as soon as they started dealing drugs to kids.

"That's fine. If you can forward it to me, I'll look into it," she said handing over her card. "Do you know if any of your students bought any drugs?"

"Yes, unfortunately two of our year elevens were caught in possession of what I believe is cannabis."

The headmistress unlocked one of her desk drawers and, using tweezers, removed two small plastic bags. Each appeared to contain what did indeed look like dope, but such a tiny amount, Jo doubted there was even enough to make a decent joint.

"Obviously the culprits will be suspended. They are waiting in Mr Husthwaite's office for their parents to arrive, if you would like to interview them. I have warned them that you have been informed and that they may face being charged with possession."

"Okay, I'll speak to them," agreed Jo a little half-heartedly. "I'll need a responsible adult to be there if their parents haven't arrived yet."

"I'm sure Mr Husthwaite will be happy to sit in," replied Ms Mountford as she opened the door and briskly made her way down the corridor. Jo reluctantly followed.

"You're suspending them, even though it isn't term time?" she asked.

"Yes, they will not be able to attend the holiday club and they'll also miss the first two weeks of term. It may sound harsh, Sergeant, but we have a very clear anti-drugs policy. The same goes for any student caught smoking or with alcohol."

Jo nodded. She knew the drill, having been suspended from school herself for repeatedly being caught smoking.

"While we are on that particular subject," continued the head teacher, "I was wondering if you'd have time to join us for one of our assemblies. Each term we like to tackle a difficult subject. This term we'll be focusing on the danger of drugs. I'm sure the children would like to hear from you."

Jo managed not to shudder again at the thought of speaking in front of a load of bored schoolkids. Instead, she attempted a look of regret. "I'm probably going to be tied up looking into this, but I can pass your request on to the school liaison team."

They arrived outside a door and Ms Mountford knocked briskly before entering. She introduced Jo to the PE teacher and Toby and Andrew—the two sixteen-year-olds—before disappearing back to her own office. The boys were both tall and thin with floppy dark hair falling across their pale, worried faces and were still dressed in their school football strip. Mr Husthwaite was a short, tubby man with grey hair. He was wearing a green tracksuit and looked even more upset than his pupils. Ironically hanging behind him on the wall was a photo of several students including Toby and Andrew receiving their Silver Duke of Edinburgh awards.

"I haven't been able to check if either of you have any previous convictions. Can you tell me if you've been in trouble with the police before?" she began, although she was fairly sure she knew the answer.

"No," replied Toby immediately.

"Never," confirmed Andrew. "My mum and dad are going to kill me."

"They've always been good lads," added Mr Husthwaite. "We are expecting them to get decent grades in their GCSEs and both of them have represented the school and the county in football and cross-country."

Jo nodded politely before turning back to the two boys. "What can you tell me about the guy you bought the dope from?"

"Nothing really. We'd seen him hanging about before," replied Toby.

"But this was the first time we'd bought anything," interjected Andrew quickly. "We just wanted to try it. See what all the fuss was about."

"That's right," agreed Toby. "I'd say he's in his late twenties. He's about five foot eight or nine, and he's got a buzz cut and a Leeds accent." He paused for a second. "And he's got a tattoo on his neck."

"What sort of tattoo?"

"Like a lightning bolt. And I think his name might be Darren." Toby paused again. "I overheard someone calling him Daz."

"He was driving an Audi TT, electric blue with a dual exhaust and whitewall tyres," added Andrew.

"That's very precise," replied Jo as she noted down all the

information.

"Andrew knows a lot about cars. He wants to be a mechanical engineer," explained the PE teacher with a hint of pride in this voice.

"Did either of you see him selling to other students before today?" she asked. The two boys exchanged a worried glance.

"It's okay," Jo assured them. "I'm not going to ask you to name any of your friends, but I need to know if he has regular customers in the area. If it's likely he'll come back here again."

"Yeh, I guess you could say he has a few regular customers in town, or at least I think he does," replied Toby cautiously.

Jo nodded. They both looked like they were about to throw up but were trying their best to be helpful. It was obvious they had simply made a stupid decision and now they were paying for it. It was time to put them out of their misery.

"I see," she said slipping her electronic notebook into her pocket, "well as far as I'm concerned this is the end of the matter."

"Really!" both boys and Mr Husthwaite exclaimed in unison.

"Yes," confirmed Jo allowing herself a small smile, "this is your first offence and the amount involved is too small to result in a prosecution, but let this act as a warning. If you are caught in possession again, you'll be arrested and at the very least be cautioned if not charged—and that means a criminal record. Do you understand?"

"Yes," replied both the boys in stereo again.

"Thank you," added Toby.

Jo made her way to the door. "Good luck, lads, and don't take this the wrong way, but I really hope I don't see you again."

WHEN SHE RETURNED to the station it was after five and most of her colleagues had gone home. She got herself a coffee from the machine and spent the rest of the evening signing off reports to send to the Crown Prosecution Service regarding the case against Guy. When she'd finished, she looked at the photos the PE teacher had taken and the head had emailed to her. They were a bit blurred, but they showed a stocky white guy with a shaved head. On one it was possible to see the tattoo Toby had mentioned. A thought suddenly occurred to her. One of the children who'd seen the man hanging around outside Hartwell's school had said he had a zigzag on his neck.

MEERA HAD CALLED in a panic when Rachel had told her about him. Jo could cheerfully have strangled Rachel for not keeping her mouth shut, but then the two of them often didn't see eye to eye. According to Meera, it was because they were too similar.

"You both fly off the handle too quickly," she had tutted on more than one occasion. Meera hardly ever lost her cool, but she could worry for England, which was why Jo had said they shouldn't mention the stranger to her. They only had a couple of vague descriptions from two seven-year-old boys and neither of them could agree if the man had asked about Krish by name or just enquired about 'an Indian kid'. Now Jo wondered whether it was possible the guy with the tattoo was trying to push drugs in Hartwell. Anger surged through her. What sort of a creep targeted primary school kids?

Returning to the photographs she zoomed in on one showing the car. If she squinted, it was possible to make out the registration number. She quickly entered the details on the central database. As she expected it had been reported stolen a couple of days before. No doubt the dealer kept changing his car to avoid detection. She checked where the car had been taken from. It was a Leeds address. She decided to send the photo of the guy to a contact she had in West Yorkshire Police. She also emailed over the description of the tattoo and the possibility that his name was Darren. Maybe they would be able to identify him.

Jo checked her watch and yawned. She doubted she'd hear anything tonight, but if West Yorkshire confirmed he was a known dealer, she might be able to persuade her bosses to set up a surveillance operation to catch him. It wasn't the complex sort of investigation she'd been involved with in London, but one more dealer off the streets could only be a good thing.

IT WAS LATE when she returned home that night. Meera's

cottage was in darkness. Her neighbour must have gone to bed already. Jo was tempted to go to the pub. She wasn't especially hungry, but Jack would be there. It would be nice to see a friendly face. Then she decided against it. Her hip was still sore from when she'd fallen off the stepladder in Mary's kitchen. Soaking in a hot bath with a cold beer might be a better idea.

Before she fell asleep, she scrolled through the headlines on the *Evening Standard* website. She couldn't shake the habit of checking what was happening in London. Even if she didn't live there anymore, it was definitely more interesting than reading about the price of sheep that seemed to fill the pages of the local paper here in Yorkshire.

Her eyes scanned the screen. There was the usual stuff about congestion charges going up and tube strikes, until something caught her attention. There was a report of an armed robbery. Not many details were given, but a pair of shotguns had been used and the names of the two men who had been arrested. Kyle Gorton and Ryan Kelly. Jo recognised them immediately. They were part of Roy Sutcliffe's drugs gang. She and her team had been targeting him before she'd messed up the arrest of their leader and been sent up north. She read through the report again, but there was no more information.

With a sigh, she closed her laptop. Whatever they'd been up to, she wouldn't be able to find out until she read about it in another newspaper report like everyone else. Instead, she was stuck in Hartwell trying to track down a small-time dope dealer.

CHAPTER SIX

LUCY LET OUT a howl of frustration, which immediately caused Pickle, the Jack Russell, and Root, the puppy, to begin barking in sympathy. Tilly, the black Labrador, merely raised an eyebrow and sighed heavily, as if to say they should all know better.

"Why don't you ask Mr Bradbury to go over it with you again, love? I'm sure he wouldn't mind," suggested Joan sympathetically. She was busy making sandwiches and quiches for the film crew who were working upstairs. Lucy shook her head as she stuffed the spreadsheets back into their folder. There was no way she could handle another meeting with the well-meaning but mind-numbing accountant.

"No, he'll confuse me even more. I'm going to see if Rachel will give me a hand. She does the farm's accounts for her mum. Do you mind keeping an eye on Freddie while I pop out? I don't want him getting in the way of the film crew. Meera's collecting him for a sleepover with Krish, when she finishes work, but I'm not sure when," she called over her shoulder as she headed out of the door.

She tried Rachel's mobile, but there was no answer. She drove down into the village, but there was no sign of her at the farm or her cottage. Lucy wondered if it was possible she'd gone for a ride on Bailey, her old pony. She decided to pop into the pub and see if anyone there knew.

"Luce! I haven't seen you in here for a while. Are you and Freddie okay?" asked Jack with a broad grin as soon as he saw her.

"We're good thanks, Jack. Is Rachel around? I was hoping she would help me with the estate's accounts. I know she does the farm's. I've tried her cottage and her mobile, but there was no answer from either."

"She's on holiday. She got a last-minute deal to somewhere in Italy, I think."

"Really?" said Lucy in surprise. "She didn't tell me." There was a time when she thought they told each other everything. She sighed. "I don't suppose you know anything about accounts do you, Jack? Now Freddie has officially inherited from Rupert, there's loads to sort out and quite honestly, it feels like I'm drowning in spreadsheets."

Jack shook his head sympathetically. "No sorry, Lucy. Mum does our books. I'm sure she'd help, but she's taken herself off for some retail therapy in Harrogate with Mary."

"I'll take a look if you want."

Lucy spun around. Sitting at a table in the far corner, reading the newspaper, was Rob. Lucy hadn't noticed him when she'd first walked in. She felt her face flush. They had barely spoken since the night Guy was arrested.

"That's kind of you. Are you sure you aren't too busy?" she replied and cringed at the stammer in her voice.

Rob rose to his feet and fixed those intense blue eyes of his on her face.

"I wouldn't have offered if I was," he replied evenly.

Feeling flustered at the thought of being on her own with him, she couldn't think of a reason to turn down his offer without sounding rude, so instead she smiled.

"Okay, thanks. That would be great."

"SO, WHAT'S THE verdict? Are we really broke? Are Freddie and I going to end up out on the streets?"

The two of them were sitting on either side of the kitchen table. Sheets of figures were spread out between them. Rob's lips twitched into a smile at her dramatic tone and shook his head.

"Hardly. You are asset rich, even if some of those assets are carrying hefty mortgages, but you do have a serious cash flow problem. It would help if you focused where you spend more sensibly. You see you've invested in these two properties, but they currently don't bring in any income. The money would have been better spent elsewhere," he explained, pushing the two balance sheets he'd been studying across the table to her. Lucy frowned as her eyes scanned the figures.

"I don't understand," she murmured.

Rob tapped the sheet of paper with his finger. "You've spent almost five grand on those two properties, but they are currently empty. Instead, you could have spent the money here at the Hall, continuing the renovations. With all the bookings you've got this summer, this place is going to be your biggest income generator."

"No, I get that," said Lucy, still frowning. "I mean, the

two properties listed here, Netherby Heights and Moorhead Farm, they have been empty for years. Nobody wants to rent them because they are so remote and the land up there is almost impossible to farm, but I was up there only last week. Freddie and I took the dogs up there for a long walk. Neither place looked like they'd had any work done to them."

"Are you sure?" asked Rob.

"Absolutely. Occasionally, shooting parties would use them as shelter if the weather turned. I was last up there eighteen months ago, and when I saw them last week, they looked worse if anything."

Rob began to rifle through the papers again until he found two invoices.

"The work for those two properties was approved by Max. Maybe you should get in touch with him and see what he has to say about all this," suggested Rob. His tone was serious. Lucy knew he didn't have a very high opinion of her estate manager.

"I can't. He and Becky have taken Araminta to Florida. They aren't back until this evening, I think."

Rob leaned back in his chair. He was silent for a moment. "Look," he said, sounding cautious, "I'm not saying you don't know your properties, but maybe I should drive up there and take a look. It says here improvements to roof and exterior, which is a bit vague, but I'll soon be able to tell if any building work has been done in the last couple of months."

"Okay, good idea," agreed Lucy standing up and reaching for her coat.

"Are you coming too?" asked Rob, sounding surprised.

"Of course I am. I want to come and see for myself what's been going on. It's about time I paid more attention to the whole estate, not just the Hall. Why would you think I'd want to stay behind?"

Rob stuck his hands in his jeans pockets and looked at the floor. It seemed like he wanted to say something, but eventually he simply shrugged. "Okay then, but we'll take my car. I'm not sure yours will make it up there," he said collecting his keys and heading out the door.

"Dizzy is a four-wheel drive too," protested Lucy, hurrying after him. Rob looked over his shoulder and grinned at her.

"It's also knackered, Luce. Even if it made it up there, I bet it wouldn't make it back."

"Okay you might have a point," she agreed, but the idea of being stuck on the moors with Rob Harrison didn't seem too terrible at all.

ROB DROVE THEM up to the moors behind the village. The two farms could only be reached by winding, potholed tracks. They sat in silence as the pickup truck bumped along. Lucy always felt uncomfortable not talking, but it didn't seem to bother Rob, who hummed quietly along to the radio. After a while Lucy began to relax too.

They arrived at Moorhead Farm first. Lucy jumped out to open the rusty iron gate into the farmyard while Rob drove through. The farmhouse was long and thin and made of stone. The two of them began to walk around the outside, but it was obvious that no work had been carried out. The windows and doorframes were all warped where the white paint had flaked off over the years.

"This place hasn't been touched in ages," said Rob shaking his head.

"Maybe there was a mix-up with the invoices. Perhaps all the work was done at Netherby," Lucy suggested hopefully.

"Let's take a look then," said Rob as he held the door of the pickup open for her.

However, it was the same story when they arrived at Netherby Heights a couple of miles farther down the track. It was a single-storey stone farmhouse and according to the invoice on file the roof slates had recently been replaced. Lucy walked backwards, shielding her eyes from the sun to try and see, while Rob hauled himself up on to the top of his truck.

"None of these slates have been replaced, Lucy," he shouted down. "There are quite a few missing and almost all of them are cracked."

"It's certainly been neglected," agreed Lucy. "No wonder we haven't been able to rent it out for years. It's such a shame. The view up here is breathtaking and it's so peaceful." She sighed as she leaned against the crumbling drystone wall and looked out across the moors to Hartwell nestled below.

"It is," agreed Rob as he walked over to join her.

"I don't know why you thought I wouldn't want to come up here."

"I didn't think you'd want to be alone with me somewhere where Joan isn't popping in and out every couple of minutes and there isn't a film crew working upstairs."

Lucy couldn't think of anything to say except, "Oh."

Rob turned to look at her, his face serious. "That night with Guy, you seemed scared of me. I know I overreacted and I'm sorry."

Lucy felt herself flush as she remembered that night and how Rob found out she'd suspected him of being her stalker and how she'd flinched when he'd stepped towards her. She opened her mouth to speak, but Rob held up his hand.

"I was upset that you were frightened of me," he continued, as if he was picking his words carefully, "but I understand. You'd had a tough time with Rupert, and you knew I'd been to prison. I don't blame you for thinking the worst, but I want you to know I wouldn't hurt you for the world, Lucy."

Those deep blue eyes felt like they were boring into her. She felt her mouth go dry and looked away.

"I was the one who overreacted," she said. "It wasn't you I should have been cowering from, but I was a nervous wreck. Look, can we agree not to talk about that night? To be honest, I hate to even think about it."

Rob's jaw tightened. "I hope they lock him up and throw away the key, for what he put you through."

Lucy pushed her hair away from her face and shook her head. "According to Jo, it looks like he won't even have to stand trial."

"What? That's crazy! He should pay for what he did," said Rob sounding outraged, but Lucy only shrugged her shoulders.

"It's to do with some legal reason or other. Jo tried to

explain, but I didn't understand or maybe I didn't really want to listen. The important thing is he isn't coining back here, and I won't have to give evidence in front of him." She paused. "Can we please put that night behind us and make a fresh start? Okay?"

"Okay," agreed Rob with a smile.

THEY DROVE BACK in silence. Lucy flicked through the papers in the folder she'd brought with her. She was trying to work out what had been going on at the two empty farmhouses and what else she might have missed, but it wasn't easy to concentrate when Rob's arm kept brushing against her whenever he changed gear. She caught a glimpse of his tattoo peeping out beneath the sleeve of his T-shirt. He'd told her about getting it when he'd left prison. He'd been locked up for assaulting his sister's abusive boyfriend, but he was wrong to think Lucy would hold this against him. As far as she was concerned, he'd paid his debts and been honest about the mistakes he'd made. She wished she could have said the same about all the other men in her life.

They eventually rumbled back up the drive to Hartwell Hall.

"Would you like to come in for a coffee?" she asked.

"No thanks. I need to get back to the Hayloft. I want to check on the guys burying the electric cables."

"I thought you did that weeks ago."

Rob shook his head ruefully. "We can't put them where we wanted to since we dug up those Druids. That archaeologist from York thinks there might be more to find in the field behind the house. I promised her we'd bury the cable the other side of the road, but it's taking forever." He paused. "I was wondering if you'd like to go out for dinner one night?"

Lucy's heart sank as she shook her head. "That's really kind, but to be honest, I don't feel like going out anywhere at the moment. Not just with you," she added quickly, hating the thought of offending him when he'd been so kind. "I mean I don't feel like socialising. That's why I've been taking Freddie and the dogs up on the moors for these long walks. I keep telling myself the exercise is good for them, but really it's to avoiding seeing anyone."

Rob raised his eyebrows as she rattled on.

"It's okay, Lucy. I get it. It's fine. I know what's it's like to have the village gossiping about you. Maybe I could call in sometime instead. See how you are getting on with the accounts."

"That would be great. Thanks," she replied with a relieved smile. She climbed out of the pickup and gave him a wave goodbye before entering the kitchen where she was greeted by the three dogs who were delighted to see her. There was a note on the table from Joan, telling her that the film crew had left for the day and that Meera had collected Freddie. She filled the kettle and put it on top of the Aga. As she waited for it to boil, she wondered if she should have accepted Rob's invitation. She shook her head as she spooned some instant coffee into her mug. If she'd learnt one thing over these last few years, it was that her judgement, particularly when it came to men, wasn't to be trusted. Plus, she had more than enough going on trying to get to grips with running the estate. The last thing she and Freddie needed was another man messing up their lives—she was more than capable of doing that herself.

As she poured the boiling water into the mug, there was a loud jangling from the old bell board above the kitchen door. Lucy looked up and frowned. It was the front door. For a second, she wondered whether Rob had come back; but no, he wouldn't use the front door. Maybe one of the film crew had forgotten something. She made her way down the corridors and through the main hall with the three dogs woofing loudly as the bell continued to jangle.

"All right, all right, I'm coming," she muttered to herself, as she pulled back the bolts and turned the key in the lock, before heaving the heavy front door open. She froze. Standing beneath the portico was a woman Lucy hadn't seen since she was a teenager, but with her shaggy blonde mane held back with a huge pair of sunglasses and her big blue eyes ringed with smudged kohl, she was unmistakable.

"Darling!" the woman declared, letting the smouldering Marlboro light fall from her fingers before throwing her arms around Lucy's neck. "It's wonderful to see you!"

"Hello, Mum," replied Lucy cautiously returning the hug. "What are you doing here?"

Her mother stepped back and looked at her in surprise.

"Why, darling, I had to come as soon as I heard the terrible news. It was in all the papers. Even in Cape Town, you made the front pages. First that creepy old MP stalking you and then poor Rupert being found in a cave. Such a shame! You must be totally devastated, but don't worry, Mummy is here to help."

"Thank you," said Lucy, weakly. All of a sudden, she felt like a little girl again, although she'd never called the woman on her doorstep 'Mummy'. In fact, her mother had practically forbidden it, instead Lucy had always been encouraged to call her Sadie. Sadie March had become famous as a model and party girl. She had made the front pages plenty of times herself, usually on the arm of whoever happened to be at the top of the charts that week. Her brief and unexpected marriage to a handsome stockbroker had resulted in Lucy, but she had soon grown bored of being a wife and mother and had left them both when Lucy was barely two years old.

She'd run off with an Australian rock star ten years her junior and Lucy had barely had any contact with her except for cards at Christmas and birthdays and the occasional stilted long-distance phone call. Since the Australian, there had been a long list of international boyfriends, usually musicians, occasionally actors, but always a famous name.

"Well, aren't you going to invite me in, darling?" asked Sadie, interrupting Lucy's thoughts.

Lucy smiled. "Of course, please come in," she said, then noticing the two large suitcases behind her mother: "Let me give you a hand with those."

"Thanks, darling. That's terribly kind of you," replied Sadie as she breezed past Lucy and pushed away the barking dogs, who were eager to sniff the new arrival. "By the way, sweetie, could you take care of the driver for me? I was in such a rush to get here, I completely forget to change my rand to sterling."

Lucy dashed down the steps to pay the waiting taxi before lugging the first heavy case through the door. She found Sadie casting a critical eye over the great hall with its black-and-white marble flooring and the walls with huge oil paintings of Rupert's ancestors.

"I have to say, you've done very well for yourself, darling," she said, flashing Lucy a dazzling smile.

"How long are you planning on staying?" asked Lucy, as she heaved the second case inside and closed the door behind her with a heavy thud.

"For as long as you need me. Why aren't you pleased to have me here?" Sadie turned to look at Lucy with a sad expression.

"Of course, I am. But it's such a surprise seeing you," replied Lucy quickly, stopping herself just in time from adding *after all this time*.

Sadie stepped forward and took Lucy by the shoulders. "Let me look at you properly, darling."

Lucy squirmed with embarrassment. Sadie always made her feel this way. Like an awkward gauche teenager, whose appearance was being evaluated by someone far more sophisticated. She turned away, not wanting to hear her mother's verdict.

"Come on through into the library," she said instead. "You must be thirsty after your journey. Can I get you a tea or a coffee?"

Sadie following Lucy and the dogs into the library, where she flopped down on to one of the large, squishy, slightly worn velvet sofas.

"That sounds awfully dull, darling. Surely this is a cause for celebration. Let's open a bottle of bubbly."

"Oh, I'm sorry. I don't think I have any in the fridge."

"Now that's a problem that can be easily remedied. I'm sure a wonderful house like this has an amazing cellar. Am I right, darling?"

Lucy smiled despite herself. It looked like Sadie would never stop being a party girl.

"You are. I'll go and see what I can find."

A few minutes later, Lucy returned from the dark and dusty cellars with two bottles of champagne and found her mother examining the silver framed photos that covered the antique mahogany table. She was holding the only picture Lucy had of herself with both her parents. It was a black-and-white artistic shot. No doubt taken by one of Sadie's fashionable photographer friends. Lucy was about a year old. She was wearing a long white dress and had a mass of blonde curls. Both she and her father were staring adoringly at Sadie, who in turn was pouting seductively into the camera.

"Gosh this seems like an awfully long time ago doesn't it, darling?" she said returning the photo to its place. "And don't tell me this handsome chap is my grandson? He looks terribly grown-up." Lucy, after a slight struggle, managed to open the champagne with a satisfying pop. She glanced over to her mother who was now looking at a photo of Freddie, taken on his first day of school.

"Yes, that's Freddie. But that photo was taken a few years ago," she replied, not able to keep the edge out of her voice. It wasn't lost on Sadie.

"Oh dear. I haven't been much of a mother or a grand-mother, have I? I would like to see him though."

"He's staying with a friend tonight," explained Lucy,

handing her mother a glass of champagne. "What shall we drink to?"

"To us, darling."

The two women clinked glasses. Sadie took a long drink, before turning her attention back to Freddie.

"He's going to be a real ladykiller by the looks of things. How is he? I mean, how is he coping with losing his father?"

"As well as can be expected," replied Lucy. She really didn't feel like discussing her son with someone who had never met him and could barely remember to send him a birthday card. Sadie sank back down on to the sofa and looked thoughtful.

"To think your little boy is Lord Hanley now. I mean that is how it works isn't it? He inherits even though he's only a child?"

"Yes, Freddie inherited everything. Naturally, I'll have to try and take care of everything until he's old enough to run things himself."

"Gosh! That sounds like an awful lot of hard work." Sadie drained her glass. "And what about you, darling? How are you? I have to say, you seem to be coping terribly well with being a widow."

"Well, Rupert disappeared a long time ago. I suppose I got used to him not being around."

Sadie patted the cushion next to her and put her head on one side. "Tell me all about it."

Reluctantly, Lucy joined her and shrugged again. "There really isn't much to say. Rupert disappeared before the lockdown and they finally found his body in a cave not far from here."

"And the MP? I read he threatened you with a gun."

Lucy felt a shiver go through her. It was in this very room that she'd managed to get away from Guy, thanks only to Rob, Jo and Jack.

"I misjudged him," she said simply. "It seems that's always been rather a problem for me. Misjudging people, particularly men."

"I expect having someone around to advise you would have helped," said Sadie softly. "Or maybe just to offer an ear to listen."

Lucy didn't reply. Sadie put her glass down and stared at Lucy intently.

"I know I might not have always been the mother you would have liked, Lucinda, but I have always loved you. Give me a chance to make things up to you. You have been through such a lot. Let me try and help. Let me behave like a real mother for once. This could be a new start for both of us." She took Lucy's hands in her own. "I wasn't there for the parents' evenings or for helping with homework and quite honestly, darling, I wouldn't have been any good at that sort of thing. Children need structure in their lives and that simply isn't me. I could barely get myself to photo shoots on time, let alone take care of a baby. But if there is one thing I do know about, it's men. Please, darling, tell me all about it. Let me finally be of some use to you."

Lucy stared back at Sadie's face, so full of concern. How many times over the years had she wanted to hear these words? Wanted her mother to be there for her. She felt tears begin to well up in her eyes. Before she knew it all came pouring out. She told Sadie everything. How Rupert had changed after she'd given birth to Freddie. At first, just being distant, but as his drug use increased becoming more violent. Then everything about Guy too. How she thought she could trust him, that he was a friend, only to find he was totally unhinged and had been spying on her. When she'd finished, it was well after midnight. They were both exhausted from the crying, the hugging and the champagne.

Lucy installed Sadie in what used to be her mother-in-law's bedroom, kissed her goodnight and made her way a little unsteadily to her own room. That second bottle of champagne was starting to feel like a mistake. She fell into her bed with the room spinning. As she closed her eyes, she thought about Sadie and what she'd said. Maybe after all these years, this really could be a new start for them both.

Sadie spent most of the next day in bed. Lucy put it down to jet lag. She took her a cup of tea upstairs mid-morning, but Sadie remained under the covers and dismissed her with a wave of her hand. She finally surfaced in the late afternoon, not long after Lucy had picked Freddie up from Meera's.

"We have a guest," Lucy explained to him. "Your other granny is staying with us for a while."

"My other granny? You mean your mum?" queried the little boy, who had only ever seen photographs of his maternal grandparents.

"That right. Let's go and meet her."

They found Sadie wearing a silky kimono, lounging on a sofa in the library and sipping a glass of Chianti Lucy had been planning to use when she cooked spag bol that evening.

"Hello, Mum," said Lucy thinking how strange it felt to

use that word. "This is Freddie, your grandson."

"Hello, Granny," said Freddie, politely holding out his hand.

"My goodness aren't you handsome! Now come and sit down next to me and tell me all about yourself." Sadie laughed, ruffling Freddie's hair as she refilled her glass. "And call me Sadie, darling. Granny makes me feel ancient."

Lucy smiled to herself as she left the room. Some things never changed.

CHAPTER SEVEN

"WHAT DO YOU think, Meera?" Ben whispered in her ear. The enthusiastic estate agent had finally left them in peace for a moment, while he went in search of the keys for the new back door that had been swiftly replaced following the visit from Jo and her colleagues.

Meera was aware that she'd barely spoken since they'd arrived, but the Grange had quite simply taken her breath away. It was the sort of place she'd fantasised about living in when her father had first told her they were moving to England. It might not be as grand as Hartwell Hall, but the elegantly proportioned rooms, sweeping staircase, open fires and panelled walls were worthy of being in any of the Brontë or Austen novels Meera had devoured.

"Meera?" repeated Ben. She turned to look at him, blinking back tears. His face creased in concern. "What's wrong? Don't you like it? Don't get upset. There are plenty of other places we can look at."

"I love it," she replied breathlessly. "I absolutely love it."

Ben grinned back at her. "Really? Me too! You don't mind the décor? It's really not your style. Plus, some rooms are a bit scruffy and I know you like things to be perfect."

Meera glanced around them. It was true the colour

schemes and furniture were a little dated, but she could see past all that. Mentally she had already repainted the walls in various shades from Farrow and Ball, rolled up the heavily patterned carpet and polished the floorboards beneath until they gleamed. Her own collection of simple pencil drawings and watercolours would replace the gilt-framed sporting pictures and the ugly fringed lampshades would make way for simple, elegant light fittings. She turned back to Ben.

"When we've finished it will be perfect. Our perfect family home," she declared confidently.

"Shall I go and tell the agent we want to make an offer at the price we discussed?"

Meera nodded and Ben gave her a quick kiss before striding purposefully out the door.

"Good luck," she called after him. She remained behind in the drawing room. She was far too nervous to take part in the negotiation. Through the window she could see Krish playing on the stepping stones that led across the pond in the centre of the large garden. Once he had laid claim to the bedroom he wanted, he had begged to be allowed to go outside to explore. She tapped lightly on the window, and he turned around and waved. Then he started pointing to the water and shouting. On the other side of the glass, Meera managed to make out the words 'tadpoles' and 'newts'.

She smiled and waved back while whispering to herself, "Please be careful you don't fall in."

The constant worrying was the only thing she didn't enjoy about being a mother. When he was a baby, Krish seemed to have been constantly in and out of hospital due to his many allergies. Since moving to Hartwell he'd been much better, and she'd started to relax a little. That was until Rachel had told her about the strange man asking about Krish. Ben and Jo had both tried to reassure her that it was still safe to send him to the holiday club, but she couldn't shake the fearful feeling that always seemed to hang over her.

She turned away from the window at the sound of quick heavy footsteps and a few seconds later Ben reappeared. His happy, proud face told her he had good news.

"The agent said he had been instructed to accept any offers at the asking price, so the matter is now in the hands of our solicitors," he announced, sounding almost triumphant.

"It's ours?" asked Meera, not quite able to believe it.

"It's ours," confirmed Ben with a grin as he joined her at the window and wrapped his arm around her. Meera leaned back against him, sighing contentedly with her head resting on his chest. Then she felt her heart begin to pound as doubts crept into her mind. Rachel's slightly harsh assessment of her character had been correct. At work she was fine, but this always happened when she was making a big decision in her personal life. When she was younger, she had always done as her parents wanted without question, but this meant that as an adult, the responsibility of making a choice herself often made her anxious.

"You don't think we should have taken professional advice before putting an offer in?" she asked quietly.

"I don't think so. I've been studying the market for a while and this seems like a fair price and we can say our offer is subject to survey. I also spoke to Rob about what we were thinking. He knows far more about property than me, but he agreed the asking price was sensible. In fact, he even said if we decided not to go ahead, he might put an offer in himself."

Meera turned around in a panic. "Really? You don't think he will do you?" Rob could easily afford to pay far more than them, but Ben shook his head.

"No, not if he knows we want it. He's a good friend. He would only want the place as another project, not to turn it into a home. But he did give me the name of a surveyor he uses. We can ask him to take a look at the place while the solicitors are handling the paperwork, to be sure we don't get any nasty surprises when we move in."

"But what happens if someone else puts an offer in?" Now she knew the Grange might actually be hers she couldn't bear the thought of losing it.

"They won't," he reassured her. "We are the first people to view. The agents know we are cash buyers with nothing to sell, and we know Guy wants a quick sale. I bet contracts will be ready to sign, by the time I return from France."

"Do you still have to go to France?" Meera almost wailed. In all the excitement about the Grange, she'd almost forgotten about the trip he and some other vets had organised. They were due to leave that evening.

"Yes," he insisted with a smile, "I want to visit some of their beef producers and see if I can learn anything that will benefit my clients. It's only for two weeks and thanks to the wonders of modern technology, you, the solicitors and the agents will be able to contact me if necessary."

Meera knew he was teasing her and opened her mouth to speak again, but Ben bent his head down and silenced her with a kiss.

"I'll go to France; the solicitors will sort out the contracts and all you have to do is start packing and try very hard not to worry so much."

WHEN THEY FINALLY left the Grange after another tour around, when Meera took what felt like a thousand photos as well as copious notes and measurements, Ben suggested that the three of them had lunch at the Hart to celebrate.

"Congratulations!" said Jack as he brought their drinks to a table outside the front of the pub where they had found Jo already sunning herself. "I hope you'll all be very happy in your new home."

"Cheers!" said Jo clinking her bottle of beer against Meera's glass of mineral water then lowering her voice. "Where's Krish?"

Meera looked puzzled. "He's in the beer garden playing with Baxter until the food arrives. Why?"

"Because I have more good news for you. I think I've identified the guy hanging around outside the school. I sent his description to a colleague in Leeds, and they identified him as a small-time drug dealer. Apparently, he often targets schools and youth clubs."

"Oh, my goodness! A drug dealer here in Hartwell." Meera gasped. She'd hoped she'd left such dangers behind when she'd moved from the inner city. Ben reached across the table and squeezed her hand.

"It's good news, Meera. It means he wasn't looking for Krish after all. The children must have been confused. Right,

Jo?"

Jo nodded. "Yep, sounds like it and hopefully my bosses will agree to putting him under surveillance, so we'll catch him, whoever he is."

Meera let this news sink in for a second, then smiled too. Finally, one less thing to worry about.

"Come on then, are you going to tell me all about your plans for the Grange?" asked Jo.

"I would love to. But I must go and have a word with Max first," replied Meera nodding across the road. She had just spotted him walking towards the pub. In his red cords, checked shirt and yellow cravat he was hard to miss. As the estate manager, she thought it was only polite to give him as much notice as possible about her intention to leave the cottage. She left the others and hurried over the road.

"Hello there!" she called out. "Did you all have a lovely time in Florida?"

Max looked a little startled. He had obviously been deep in thought. "What? Oh yes! Excellent thank you. A little tacky for my tastes but the girls seemed to enjoy it."

"It must have been a relief to hear about Mary too. Have you been to visit her?" Meera asked as he'd come from the direction of his mother-in-law's farm, but Max shook his head firmly.

"No, no I haven't seen her today. Becky has been popping in and I have to say we are still both concerned. She still seems rather confused."

"Really?" Meera was surprised to hear this. Whenever she'd seen Mary since her appointment, she'd looked happy and relaxed and confident enough to go on trips out to

Harrogate and York, but she didn't want to start discussing a patient's health in the street. "Actually, Max, I wanted to let you know that I shall be leaving the cottage. If all goes well, Ben and I shall be moving to the Grange."

Max frowned. "That's rather a blow. You are exactly the sort of tenant we look for. Lucy will be disappointed. And we will need to get your notice in writing. Make it formal. All the info is in the contract."

With that he strode away. Meera watched him go and tutted to herself. She had always tried to be charitable about Max, especially as everyone else made fun of the way he dressed and how he tried to sound like Guy or the colonel. She had every intention of giving written notice and would it really have killed him to congratulate her on moving to the Grange?

IT WAS A little after nine o'clock that evening. Ben had already left for France. He and his colleagues were taking the overnight ferry from Hull to Zeebrugge before driving down through Belgium and into northern France. Meera sighed as she curled up on the sofa with a cup of mint tea. She was going to miss him terribly.

Krish had already gone up to bed and in the background a Mozart concerto, part of the Proms concerts from the Albert Hall, was playing quietly on the radio. On her knee were the sales particulars for the Grange. She couldn't stop looking at them. It felt like a dream to think it was going to be her home. All afternoon while Krish and Ben were playing cricket in the garden, she had sat in the shade sketching ideas for the kitchen and the drawing room. During the weekly trip to the supermarket, she'd spent a small fortune on the latest interior magazines and kept leafing through them for inspiration.

She finished her tea and was about to begin reading an article about the advantages of electric Agas, when there was a knock at her front door. She put down her magazine and listened. There was another knock, louder this time. Cautiously she stood up and made her way over to the door. Rachel was away so it couldn't be her. Jo would probably have gone to the back door. Maybe it was Lucy or a patient who needed help. There was another knock. She carefully pulled back the bolts, opened the door and froze. Her husband was standing in front of her.

"Dev! What are you doing here?"

"I need to speak to you. It's important," he said urgently. Meera stepped to one side, feeling slightly dazed as he walked past her. She closed the door behind him and followed him through into the sitting room.

"Have you got any whisky?" he asked.

"No," replied Meera. "There's wine in the fridge if you want some though."

"Thanks. Make it a large one will you?" he said flopping down on to the sofa she had recently vacated. Meera rolled her eyes as she went to fetch him a drink. Typical Dev! Turning up uninvited and expecting her to run around after him. She returned to the sitting room and handed him the glass.

"What's all this about?" she asked, taking a seat opposite

him.

Dev took a long slug of wine. He looked terrible. He was wearing a pinstriped suit but had removed his tie. His handsome face was unshaven, his eyes were bloodshot with dark rings beneath them, and it looked like he'd lost weight.

"Are you ill?" she pressed.

Dev shook his head. "No, but I need your help." He took another drink of wine. "I'm being blackmailed."

Meera stared at him. "What do you mean blackmailed? By whom?"

"Do you remember Liam?"

"Yes," replied Meera. Liam was the young man Dev had chosen to spend lockdown with rather than with his wife and son. "I thought the two of you had split up."

"We have, but I don't think I ever explained how I met him. You see, I was defending his brother Darren, who was in court on a drugs charge. After he was found innocent, Liam came over to thank me. I invited him to lunch…"

"That sounds very romantic, Dev," interrupted Meera, impatiently, "but why is he blackmailing you now?"

"He isn't. When he left me, he went out to Australia for a year. It's Darren who is blackmailing me. He has a photo that Liam must have sent him. It shows us—" he took another slug of wine "—well it's obvious we are a couple. He's threatening to send it to my parents unless I give him two grand."

Meera held up her hands to silence him. "I'm sorry, Dev, but this is your mess. You sort it out. Pay him or tell your family the truth—it's up to you. It's not my problem."

"Actually, Meera, I'm afraid it might be. You see I've already tried to call his bluff. I told him I wouldn't pay. Quite honestly, I didn't think he'd be able to track down my family in India. I never told Liam much about them, you see, but Darren didn't react very well. He said it wouldn't only be me who suffered, and he started talking about how he knew I had a little boy. He said he knew where you lived."

Meera suddenly felt very cold. Her first instinct was to rush upstairs and check her little boy was okay, but she didn't want to risk waking him up, scaring him. She flicked the radio off. Through the wall she could hear the muffled sound of shouting and gunfire. Jo must still be awake and no doubt watching one of those violent gangster thrillers she was so fond of. She reached for her mobile and hit Jo's name on her list of contacts. It began to ring and the noise from next door stopped abruptly. Jo answered.

"Jo, please can you come over?" she said trying to keep the panic out of her voice.

"Sure," replied Jo before hanging up.

"What are you doing?" demanded Dev.

"Getting some advice from an expert. My neighbour is a detective sergeant."

"Meera, I really didn't want to involve the police."

"Tough."

There was a tapping at the back door and Meera hurried to let Jo in. She brought her through to the sitting room and introduced her to Dev, who barely acknowledged her. It seemed the shock of being blackmailed had knocked all the easy charm out of him. Jo as usual was unfazed.

"What's up?" she asked.

"Dev is being blackmailed and now the man is threatening Krish," replied Meera, her words tumbling out.

"What's the blackmailer's name?" asked Jo, addressing Dev.

"Darren Prentis," he replied.

"Shaved head and a lightning bolt tattoo on his neck?" enquired Jo.

"Yes," agreed Dev, looking up in surprise.

"Do you know him?" asked Meera.

"Yep. He's the drug dealer I told you about at lunch. The guy the kids saw at the school."

"Oh my God," wailed Meera. "He's already been in the village looking for our son. A drug dealer! How could you let this happen, Dev? If you know his name and address, can you go and arrest him?"

"They can't. There isn't enough evidence," interrupted Dev, the lawyer in him suddenly kicking in. "I've deleted all his calls. I suppose I was hoping it would all go away."

Meera collapsed on to the sofa with her head in her hands. She felt Jo pat her awkwardly on the back.

"Meera, I know you're scared, but from what I've heard Darren's just a petty criminal. He hasn't got any record of violence, and kidnapping is way out of his league. I'll bet he only wanted to get a photo of Krish to send to Dev to pile the pressure on."

"We'll have to leave Hartwell," said Meera sitting up again. Mentally she was already planning where she could take her son. Maybe they could follow Ben to France or head back up to Scotland. She'd felt safe there.

Jo came and knelt down next to her. Her voice was unusually gentle. "Meera, please try and stay calm. I know you want to keep Krish safe but promise me you won't make any decisions tonight. Sleep on it and see how you feel in the morning. Very soon we'll have Darren under surveillance. Hopefully we'll get him for supplying, but if he goes anywhere near Krish, we'll know about it. If he contacts Dev again, I suggest he agrees to pay up, and we can catch him at the handover. Does that sound okay?"

Meera nodded. She knew what her friend was saying made sense, but she was still trembling.

"Okay," she whispered. They both looked at Dev who had barely spoken and was still staring into his wine glass.

"Okay," he agreed without looking up.

WHEN MEERA OPENED her eyes the next morning, she thought for a second it had all been a horrible dream, then Krish came running into her room.

"Mum, Mum. Dad's asleep on the sofa. What's happened? Where's Ben? Is Dad living with us again?"

Meera groaned. Dev had only been here a few hours and already he was confusing their son. She sat up, pushing her hair away from her face and patted the bed.

"Come and sit down, Krish."

The little boy did as she said. His face looked very serious.

"Your dad is not living with us again. He arrived last night and when we'd finished talking, it was too late for him to drive home." She didn't add that he'd also drunk far too much wine for it to be safe. "Ben is away in France, remember? He'll be home with us in two weeks' time."

At that moment, there was a strangled scream from down in the sitting room.

"Meera," yelled Dev. "Come quickly. There is a rat running about the place."

"Darwin," said Krish and Meera in unison, before both rushing downstairs to rescue Dev from the ferret.

When Krish had retrieved Darwin and Dev had recovered from his early morning encounter with his son's pet, Meera made him a strong black coffee. Then she retreated to the kitchen, but left the door ajar, so she could hear what Krish and Dev were talking about.

"You'll like Darwin when you get to know him, Dad."

"He's quite an unusual pet."

"Ben got him for me because of my allergies."

"Ben?"

"Yes. He's a vet so he knows loads about animals. When we went to Scotland, he showed me red squirrels and we saw some otters."

"Time to have a shower and brush your teeth, Krish," Meera called out from the kitchen. If Dev was going to start grilling anyone about Ben, it would be her. And right on cue as soon as she heard Krish running up the stairs, Dev appeared in the doorway looking furious.

"Who is this Ben person? How could you let a stranger take my son away on holiday?"

"Don't be ridiculous! I was with them. Ben and I are a couple."

Dev looked genuinely stunned, but Meera wasn't about to let him say a word until she'd finished speaking.

"After all your infidelities don't even think of playing the outraged husband. I have a right to a life whether you like it or not."

"Is it serious?"

"Yes, it is," replied Meera. Dev was struck dumb for a moment and Meera realised with a flash of indignation that this scenario had really never occurred to him. He had seriously never expected her to want more than their sham of a marriage.

"I still think you should have consulted me. Krish is still my son," he finally grumbled.

"Consulted you?" she snapped. "How was I meant to do that exactly, when half the time I have no idea where you are? You only contact us when it suits you or you want something. We thought you were still in India. As for Ben, I can tell you he is a good man who cares about Krish very much. Instead of thinking about him, you should concentrate on how you are going to deal with the man threatening our son."

"All right, all right. Calm down, Meera. I said I would let you know if he contacts me again. Now could I please have another coffee and a headache tablet?"

THAT EVENING WHEN Meera finished work, she went to collect Krish from Hartwell Hall where he'd spent the day with Freddie. Following Dev's visit, she hadn't dared let him go to the school holiday club. Instead, she'd phoned Lucy, who had immediately said she and Freddie would love Krish to come over. Meera knew she could relax if he was hidden away there with Lucy, Joan, Bill and now Sadie. Lucy had introduced her to her rather glamorous mother when she'd dropped Krish off.

"My goodness," said Meera as she arrived at the Hall and spotted all the film crew dashing around, "it looks terribly busy here. I hope Krish hasn't been getting under anyone's feet."

"Not at all," replied Lucy, greeting her with a hug. "He and Freddie have been down by the lake with the dogs most of the day. They occasionally appear in the kitchen when hunger strikes, otherwise I would hardly know they are here. I only wish I could say the same for my mother." She sighed. "She's been trying to chat up the leading man all afternoon."

Meera followed her friend's gaze across the courtyard to where Sadie was pouting and talking animatedly to a handsome man in a frock coat and breeches who looked vaguely familiar.

"Why don't you stay for a while?" suggested Lucy. "They've been setting up all day, but I think the cameras are finally about to roll."

Normally, Meera would have leapt at the chance to watch one of her favourite books being brought to life, but she had too many other things on her mind to be able to concentrate on Jane's problems.

"Maybe another time. I've got a bit of a headache," she replied not entirely untruthfully. Her head had felt as though there was a tight band around it since Dev had dropped his bombshell. Part of her wanted to tell Lucy what was going on, but she also didn't want to scare Krish. That was why she hadn't told Ben immediately. If he came dashing home, Krish was bound to ask why. Perhaps the fewer people who knew the better for now. Besides Lucy had enough problems of her own.

Back at the cottage she and Krish sat together in silence as they ate their tea. Meera watched her son from across the table. He had been pushing the same chunk of asparagus around his plate for the last two minutes. He had been subdued since he came home and the rims of his eyes looked sore and red, although it was possible that was down to the high pollen count.

"You're very quiet. Is something bothering you? Is it your hay fever?"

Krish shook his head. "No. I've been sneezing a bit, but I'm okay. I was thinking about Dad."

"Really?" replied Meera trying to sound casual, but she wondered where this conversation was going to lead. She and Krish rarely discussed Dev, but she often wondered if he really believed that it was simply work that kept his father away or if he ever thought about the handsome young men that sometimes strayed across the screen when Dev was Skyping them. She had tried rehearsing what she would say if Krish asked her about them, but right now if he put her on the spot, she wasn't sure if she could come up with the right words. "What were you thinking about him?" she asked, still trying to keep her tone light.

"I was thinking it isn't fair," said Krish, his face very serious. "I've got Dad, even if I don't see him much, and now I've got Ben, who I see loads. It's like I've got two dads, but Freddie hasn't even got one dad anymore."

Meera put her own knife and fork down. This wasn't what she had expected.

"Is Freddie very upset about what happened to his father?" she asked. Everyone had thought how well he was coping, but perhaps his best friend knew differently.

"I don't know. I don't think so, but he doesn't really talk about him, and then I started thinking about Jo too. She's never had a mum or a dad. It really isn't fair, is it?"

"No," Meera agreed quietly. "It isn't. But Freddie has Lucy who loves him very much and now he has both his grandmothers living in the village. As for Jo, well she's a grown-up now and has other people who care about her—like you and me."

Krish nodded, but Meera got the feeling she hadn't convinced him.

"Would you like an ice cream instead?" she asked as he continued to play with the remaining vegetables on his plate. He looked up in surprise. Meera was usually quite strict about him leaving a clean plate before eating dessert.

"Really? Yes please, Mum."

She watched as he took his choc ice out into the garden with Darwin scampering after him. His gloomy mood seemed to have lifted, but he had left Meera thinking. All this time she had fretted about what Krish was missing out on by not having Dev around much, but he'd only considered how lucky he was compared to his friends. Maybe she should follow his example. Instead of worrying about what might go wrong, she should concentrate on everything that was going right in her life.

CHAPTER EIGHT

T HE BAY OF Naples stretched out below her, so blue and
     sparkling, it almost didn't seem real. Rachel tilted her
face up towards the sun as she took another sip of her Aperol
spritzer. She'd developed quite a taste for the fizzy orange
drink since arriving in Italy. She stretched her legs out in
front of her. They were still aching from her climb to the top
of Mount Vesuvius the previous day.

She had arrived in Italy four days earlier. Naples had
been quite a shock to the system after leaving behind sleepy
little Hartwell. The noise, the smells, the crowds of people
who all seemed to be shouting at each other, the scooters
zipping through the streets and almost knocking her off her
feet every time she stepped off the pavement. This morning
she had arrived in Sorrento where the pace of life was much
calmer. She planned on spending the day relaxing and
reading about the history of the area before her trip to
Pompeii tomorrow. She was longing to see the ruins of the
ancient Roman city.

There had been no news from home, which she took to
be a good sign. In fact, the only message she'd received had
been a fairly cryptic one from Sarah. All it had said was, *I
really hope you mean that x.*

Rachel had assumed the rest of the message had been lost to some technical glitch or other. Adjusting her sunglasses, she swirled the straw around in her drink as the ice cubes clunked together. She was sitting at a table outside a bar overlooking the bay. The bar owner, a large man wearing a white apron and with the cloth he'd been using to wipe down the tables flicked over his shoulder, was chatting to a tall, distinguished gentleman with an impressive moustache. Two young boys ran past laughing as a small dog chased after them. They knocked into a crate of oranges outside one of the shops, causing the owner, a woman wearing large glasses to dash out and yell after them. Rachel smiled to herself. She'd travelled hundreds of miles, yet she could very well be watching the same scene back home in Hartwell.

At that moment, her phone began ringing from deep inside her bag. Assuming it was the tour guide confirming tomorrow's departure time, she answered without looking at the screen.

"Hi," she said, before taking another sip of spritzer.

"Oh, Rachel, thank goodness. I wasn't sure what the reception would be like out in Italy. I didn't know if I would be able to get through." Meera's voice sounded breathless at the other end of the line.

Rachel put her glass down and sat up straight. "Why? What's happened? Is it Mum?"

"Yes, but don't worry she's fine." Meera paused. "But there has been another incident."

"What sort of incident?" asked Rachel immediately, as her mind began to race. She should never have left her mum. It was selfish to have come on holiday when they still weren't sure what was wrong with her.

"It was the oven again. It seems she'd spent the morning making dough and left it to prove while she went to meet Joan, Caroline and Shirley for lunch, but there must have been a problem with the temperature because it started to burn. Fortunately, the smoke alarm you had installed alerted one of the farm workers, but Mary was very upset."

"Oh no," groaned Rachel.

"Shirley phoned me. I went up to the farm to check on Mary. As I said, she was upset, but physically okay. She didn't want me to bother you while you were on holiday, but I thought you'd want to know."

"Yes, thank you, Meera. Is she okay now? Is Becky with her?"

"I haven't seen Becky, but Joan and Shirley were still with her when I left. I thought maybe you could check the camera Jo put up."

Rachel left some euros on the table and hurried back to her hotel room so she could connect to the internet. She didn't have a laptop with her, but hopefully she could access the camera using her phone. Carefully, following the instructions Jo had given her, she logged on and found herself looking at a black-and-white image of the farmhouse kitchen. She went back to the time Meera had said Mary had left the house. Sure enough, there was her mother kneading the dough and separating it into rolls before neatly placing them on the baking tray. She wiped her hands and placed a cloth over the dough.

Rachel sat, watching and waiting, not wanting to fast-forward in case she missed something. Mary disappeared for a few moments, then returned having changed her top. She patted Jenny and left through the back door. Rachel squinted at the little screen but she couldn't see if the oven was turned on or not. Then she caught her breath as the back door opened again and in walked Max. She watched in disbelief as he casually placed the dough in the oven, fiddled with the dial, then turned and left.

She rewound the footage and watched it again. A surge of anger rose inside her. It had been Max all along. How could he? How could anyone be so cruel to her lovely mother, let alone a member of her family? Did Becky know? Rachel felt sick at the thought. She may never have got on with her sister, but it was too much to think she could be involved with what Max had been doing. No wonder they had both encouraged her to go on holiday.

Memories rushed through her head. The ideas Max kept coming up with for turning the farm buildings into holiday cottages. Becky wanting to send Araminta to a private school. The form Max had tricked her mother into signing when he was trying to get rid of Bailey, her horse. Is that what all this was about? Did Max want control of her mother's money? What else could he have got Mary to sign?

Quickly, she began googling the next available flight home. There was one that left Naples in three hours. If she set off now, she might just make it. Stuffing her things into her bag, she ran down to reception to find a taxi.

IT WAS EARLY evening when the taxi pulled up at the farmhouse. Rachel pushed open the back door. She didn't think she'd ever get the image of Max sneaking through it out of her mind.

"Rachel! What are you doing here? I wasn't expecting you until later in the week. Don't say I don't even know what day it is anymore," Mary said turning to look at the calendar where she'd neatly written 'Rachel Home'.

"No, Mum," replied Rachel gently. "You aren't confused. You never have been. That's why I came back early."

"What do you mean, love?"

"It's probably easier if I show you." She quickly set up the laptop and turned the screen towards Mary and began to play the video of Max creeping into the kitchen and fiddling with the oven. Anxiously she watched her mother's reaction, but her face remained impassive until the footage ended. Then she leaned back in her chair with a heavy sigh and a single tear trickled down her cheek. Rachel wrapped her arms tightly around her.

"Mum, I'm so sorry. I can't believe he would do this to you. I know how hurt and upset you must be."

Mary turned her head and smiled up at her.

"Do you know something, love? I just feel relieved. All this time, I've been convinced that there was something wrong with me. Now I know I'm absolutely fine and it's like a weight has disappeared from my shoulders."

Her smile faded a little. "We'll get to the bottom of what Max has been up to, but right now I want to enjoy knowing I'm not losing my mind."

Rachel folded away her laptop and watched as her mother pottered around the kitchen humming quietly to herself and shook her head. Mary might not be in a hurry for Max to explain himself, but Rachel certainly didn't share her patience. She waited as long as she could then told her mother she needed some fresh air to clear her head.

Sneaking the laptop under her jacket, she made her way to the other side of the village where her sister lived in a modern barn conversion. There was a small, wooded area across the road. She paused there and observed the house. Both Max and Becky's cars were parked on the driveway. The curtains in Araminta's bedroom were closed. Rachel checked her watch. It must be her bedtime by now. Sure enough, at that moment the light in her niece's room went out. Good. She didn't want the little girl to hear what she had to say.

Striding over to the house, she pushed open the back door without knocking and stepped inside. Becky and Max were sitting at the marble-topped kitchen table. They both looked surprised when she walked in. Becky, her tan deeper than ever, rose to her feet.

"Rachel, what are you doing here?" she asked.

"I thought you were in Italy," chimed in Max.

"Hoped I was more like," snapped Rachel.

"What's all this about, Rachel?" demanded her sister. "Max has only just got home. He's had a very busy day."

"I bet he has. It seems he's been very busy recently. Have you found another widow to frighten or do you save that sort of thing for your mother-in-law?"

"What are you talking about? You know you've got a real cheek barging in here like this," said Becky her hands on her hips, as Max smiled smugly at Rachel and shook his head.

"Calm down, Rachel. You sound quite agitated, old girl," he drawled.

"Don't old girl me. You can drop that fake bloody accent for a start," snapped Rachel, then turning back to her sister, said, "It's him. He's the one who's been making Mum think she's losing her mind. Look!"

She opened her laptop and played the video. Holding it a few inches from her sister and brother-in-law's faces.

"It was you tampering with the cooker, moving things, scaring her. How could you?" demanded Rachel.

Becky's perfectly made-up face crumpled in confusion, as she looked from the screen to her husband. "Max? What's going on?" she asked.

Max leaned back in his chair and folded his arms. It was a gesture Rachel knew he'd picked up from Rupert.

"That doesn't prove anything. I'd just popped in to check on Mary. I thought she'd forgotten to put the bread in the oven. I was trying to help," he protested.

"Don't give me that!" exclaimed Rachel. "What was the plan? Did you think you could convince her to give you control of her money and the farm? Is that why you encouraged me to go on holiday?"

Then she turned her attention back to her sister, who was still staring blankly at them both, her mouth wide open.

"Please tell me you didn't know anything about this, Becks," Rachel pleaded.

"There's nothing to know," interjected Max, who continued to smile and shake his head. "Seriously, Rachel, you've got the wrong end of the stick."

At that moment, Minty began shouting for her mother

from upstairs. Becky turned towards the door.

"I'll be back in a second. Don't say anything until I get back."

"There's nothing to say," Max called after her.

Rachel stood up as her sister disappeared through the door.

"If that's the way you want to play it, Max, that's fine. I'm going to the police. You can tell them your story. See if they believe you, because I certainly don't."

However, Max's expression had changed as soon as his wife left the room, closing the door behind her. He suddenly looked very frightened. Rachel was shocked when he reached out and grabbed her arm.

"Please, Rachel," he said in quiet, urgent voice. "You're right, I'm sorry. I should never have treated Mary in that way, but I'm in terrible trouble financially."

"What?" Rachel hissed back.

"I'm up to my neck in debt, but I've been trying to hide it from Becky. I didn't want to worry her. Please, I'm begging you. Give me until tomorrow to try and explain things to her. Tonight, when Minty is asleep, I'll sit her down. Then, tomorrow morning, if you want me to go to the police I will. I'll even put a confession in writing. Please, Rachel. It's only a few hours. I know I don't deserve it, but please for Becky and Minty's sakes."

Rachel glared at him coldly for a second before giving a curt nod. "Okay, I'll wait until the morning, but only for Becky and Minty. You make me sick."

With that she grabbed her laptop and stalked out of the kitchen.

SHE RETURNED TO the farmhouse, without telling Mary what had happened. That night she barely slept and early the next morning, she headed back to Becky's house. As she turned into the driveway, she heard the sound of footsteps jogging up behind her. It was Jo, fully dressed and looking worried.

"What are you doing here?"

"Checking up on Max and Becky. There was a report of a car being abandoned near Leeds Bradford Airport. It's registered to Max. I said I'd check it out."

"What do you mean abandoned?" asked Rachel, her heart beginning to race. Jo shrugged and peered through the small garage window.

"That's all they said. Only Becky's car is inside," she said. "Is something going on? Why are you here so early?"

"It's Max who has been making Mum think she's losing her mind. I caught him on camera interfering with the oven. I confronted him last night and he confessed."

Jo's eyes opened wide. "Wow. No wonder he's done a runner. The question is, have Becky and Minty gone too?"

Panic swept over Rachel as she ran to the back door. This time it was locked. She began pounding on it. A second later, a shocked-looking, bleary-eyed Becky opened it.

"For heaven's sake Rachel, calm down. You'll wake up Minty."

"Where is he?" demanded Rachel pushing her way inside.

"He'll be back soon," stammered Becky. She was still in

her dressing gown and without her face caked in make-up, she looked much younger and more vulnerable than usual. "Look, he told me everything last night before driving over to Manchester. He said he wanted to explain everything to his parents face to face. But don't worry, he'll be back soon. I still think this has all been a terrible mistake. Max has been under a lot of pressure recently. He knows it was wrong, but said he was sorry, and he promised me he'll make it up to Mum," then spotting Jo who had reluctantly followed Rachel inside, she said, "Really, Rachel did you have to involve the police? He's written a confession. It explains everything." She gestured towards a thick white envelope that was propped up against the fruit bowl and was address simply: 'To Whom It May Concern'.

"When did he leave?" asked Jo.

"After supper last night. Do you want a cup of tea?" asked Becky.

"No," snapped Rachel. The anger that was simmering inside her was in danger of bubbling over again.

"No thanks," replied Jo. "Has he called you since he left?"

Rachel's ears pricked up. There was something in Jo's tone that made her stop pacing up and down the gleaming white-tiled floor.

"No," replied Becky quietly, as she sank on to one of the chrome stools at the breakfast bar. She looked totally deflated, but Rachel was struggling to feel any sympathy; instead she followed Jo's gaze, which was fixed on the envelope. She reached across and picked it up.

"Have you read this?" she asked addressing her sister.

"No, but shouldn't we wait until he's here? He said it was for the police. That they would read it and probably arrest him. He knows he's done wrong, but he didn't mean to hurt anyone. He was just doing what he thought was best. He wanted to take the burden of running the farm away from Mum, convince her to let him look after everything," protested Becky weakly, her eyes filling with tears.

Rachel didn't bother to argue with her sister, but instead threw Jo a questioning glance.

"Go ahead, Rach," she replied with a shrug. Rachel tore open the envelope and unfolded the three pages covered in Max's loopy scrawl. She quickly scanned the contents and her heart began to race.

"Oh my God!" she gasped and let the pages fall from her hand as she too collapsed on to one of the bar stools. Her sister looked at her with fear in her eyes.

"What is it?" she asked. Her hand flew to her mouth. "He hasn't done something stupid has he? Please tell me it isn't a suicide note?"

Rachel slowly shook her head. For the first time since she'd seen that video of Max, she felt sorry for Becky.

Jo picked up the pages and began to read. "It's not a suicide note," she said quickly, "but it's not a confession either."

"Then what is it?" asked Becky.

Rachel turned to look at her pale, bewildered face. "The bastard's dropped you in it, Becks."

Her sister stared back at her blankly. "What do you mean?"

Jo handed the letter over. "It says here, that it was all your idea. He says your spending was out of control and he only got involved because you threatened to take Araminta away. He says he's gone abroad because he can't live with the shame," she surmised bluntly.

"No, he wouldn't do that. He wouldn't leave us. You must have got it wrong," whispered Becky, picking up the pages and reading.

"It's true, Becks," said Rachel quietly. "He even requests that Araminta goes to live with his parents, if you go to prison."

Becky stumbled from her stool and only just made it to the sink in time as she began to retch violently. Instinctively, Rachel rushed to hold her sister's hair back as she vomited again and again. She turned on the cold tap with her free hand. In the background, she could hear Jo making a telephone call, trying to find out if Max was still in the country. When Becky had finished, she splashed her face with water and began groaning quietly.

"Come and sit down," said Rachel gently, but her sister shook her head and instead slumped to the floor, her head resting against the kitchen cupboard, her face ashen. Rachel retrieved a glass from the dresser and filled it with water, but Becky pushed it away. They both looked up when Jo cleared her throat loudly.

"Max took a flight from Manchester to Malaga at eleven o'clock last night."

"He's left the country? He's really gone?" whispered Becky.

"Any idea why he'd chose Malaga?"

"His grandparents have a villa out there...or they did. I think. I can't remember."

"Can we get him back? Don't we have extradition treaties or something?" demanded Rachel.

"We probably can," replied Jo evenly. "But if he comes back and it goes to court, as things stand, it will be Becky's word against his."

"But the video, the money," protested Rachel rising from her crouched position.

"Yes, but like I said—it's clear he isn't going to confess, so there is always a risk that a court case won't go the way you want."

"Oh God, oh God," moaned Becky quietly. Rachel stared down at her, then turned back to look at her friend, as she tried to take in what she was saying. Bringing Max to justice might result in her sister being incarcerated too. What would that do to her mother?

From upstairs came a small voice. "Mummy! Mummy!"

Becky groaned from her place on the floor. "Araminta! What am I going to tell her? Please don't let her see me like this."

Jo nodded towards the door leading to the hallway. "You go. I'll stay here with Becky," she said.

Glancing back anxiously at her sister, Rachel headed out the door and up the stairs. She caught sight of herself in the huge mirror on the landing. Her forehead was creased and her mouth set in a straight line. She quickly arranged her features so she looked more relaxed and forced her lips to smile. She found Minty sitting up in her cabin bed that was designed to look like a fairy-tale castle, complete with turret. The duvet cover and curtains were covered in twirling ballerinas, and she was surrounded by a vast collection of soft toys. With her long blonde hair and big blinking eyes, she remined Rachel of Becky when she was a little girl.

"Hello, Minty. Did you sleep well?"

"Yes, thank you, Auntie Rachel. What are you doing here? Where's Mummy and Daddy?"

"Daddy has gone away for a little while and Mummy is downstairs with my friend Jo."

The little girl's face crinkled. "The one who is in the police, but doesn't wear a uniform?"

"That's right."

"Doesn't she like the uniform? Is it the colour? Would she like it if it was pink?"

"I'm not sure. I'll ask her. Now why don't I put on *Frozen* for you and I'll bring you a hot chocolate for a treat," Rachel suggested, trying to keep her tone light as she switched on the massive TV screen that was fixed to the wall opposite the bed. She found her niece's favourite film, the one she watched frequently, even in the height of summer, and gave her a quick kiss before hurrying back downstairs.

She paused briefly in the hallway in front of the picture of Max, Becky and Minty. It was a blown-up photo of the three of skiing in the Alps. The holiday before the one to Disney World. All three were grinning for the camera, but Rachel just shook her head. How had she missed it? The expensive holidays, the flash watches, the endless beauty treatments, the massive television screens. Why had she never questioned it? Had she been too busy feeling sorry for herself, rather than looking out for her mum? She jumped as the phone on the table began to ring. She picked it up.

"Hello?" she said cautiously holding the receiver to her

ear. There was silence at the other end of the phone.

"Hello?" she repeated.

"Rachel? Is that you?"

Rachel breathed a sigh of relief. It was only Lucy.

"Yes, Luce, it's me. Are you okay?"

"Yes thanks." She paused. "Actually, I was trying to get hold of Max. He's not answering his mobile."

"I bet he isn't," muttered Rachel. "Look I'm sorry, Lucy, it's a bit complicated, but we think Max has gone abroad."

There was another pause at the end of the line. "Any idea when he'll be back? It's just that I do need to talk to him quite urgently." Lucy's normal breezy, carefree voice sounded serious.

"Why? What's up?" asked Rachel.

"Um, it's a little tricky. Rob and I were looking over some of the estate accounts and well... I really wanted a word with Max."

Rachel's heart sank.

"Has he been trying to steal from you as well?" she asked bluntly. At the other end of the line she could hear a sharp intake of breath.

"Well, we have found a few discrepancies. What do you mean as well?"

Rachel shook her head. Lucy was far too polite sometimes.

"It's him who's been making Mum think she's losing the plot. He wanted to get his hands on her money and now he's disappeared to Spain. I have to go now. Becky is in a state, but I'll catch up with you later."

When Rachel stepped back into the kitchen Becky was

still slumped on the floor, but she was at least sipping a cup of tea, which Jo must have made for her. Rachel knelt down next to her sister and gave her hand a squeeze.

"Minty is fine. She's watching TV in bed. I'll take her a drink up, okay?"

Becky nodded dumbly.

"Who was on the phone?" asked Jo, who was leaning against the dresser and flicking through a pile of papers.

"Lucy. She was trying to track down Max." Rachel glanced over her sister's head to her friend. "It seems she's found discrepancies in the estate accounts."

Jo raised an eyebrow in response. "It sounds like he's been a very busy boy," she murmured.

"What have you got there?" asked Rachel.

"Credit card statements. I found them stuffed in the back of a drawer when I was looking for a teaspoon," replied Jo shaking her head. "Bloody hell, I'd bugger off too if I owed this much."

Rachel went and peered over Jo's shoulder, then caught her breath.

"They owe over twenty grand. And look at the interest they've racked up!" she hissed. They both looked over to where Becky was still rocking quietly on the floor.

"Look," said Jo quietly, "I should probably be going. Let me know if you or your mum want to bring formal charges against Max, but like I said it could get messy." She glanced over to Becky again. "I'm not an expert but you might want to get Meera to take a look at her."

However, it wasn't Meera who brought Becky out of her stupor, but Mary. When Jo had left the two sisters alone,

Rachel quickly phoned their mother and explained what had happened. Mary had hurried over. As soon as Becky saw her mother, she staggered to her feet and broke into noisy sobs.

"There now. It will be all right. Why don't you and Minty come home, love," Mary had said enveloping her younger daughter in her arms. "Let me and your sister look after you."

CHAPTER NINE

J O WAS THE first to arrive at the White Hart. Lucy had asked them all to meet up there. She wanted to introduce them to her mother, who seemed to have turned up out of the blue. Meera had already told Jo she couldn't make it. She was a bundle of nerves since Dev's visit and there was no way she would leave Krish with a babysitter for the evening. After Max's disappearance, she didn't know if Rachel would turn up either. Gossip had already started circulating around the village. Jo hoisted herself on to one of the bar stools and a second later a perfectly chilled bottle of Stella was on the bar in front of her.

"You see what a great boyfriend I would make. I anticipate your every need," said Jack with a wink. For once he was dressed smartly and had abandoned his customary rugby shirt.

"It's like you're psychic," she replied taking a swig. "What's with the tie?"

"It's my old England rugby tie. I thought I should make an effort. You know seeing as we're meeting Lucy's mum for the first time. I wanted to make a good impression. We can't have her thinking we're all scruffy sods just because we live out in the sticks." He nodded at the three old farmers to his left in their flat caps and work boots. "After all she was quite famous in her day."

"Famous! Notorious more like!" tutted Nora who was sitting at the table closest to the bar. Jack and Jo both ignored her.

"How come you've never met her before? Didn't she come to Lucy's wedding or see Freddie when he was born?"

"Nope and I've never really heard Lucy talk about her. I remember her dad came in here once or twice for a drink. He seemed like a nice chap, but he died when Freddie was still a baby."

At that moment Lucy walked through the door with a woman who could only be her mother. Shorter and older than her daughter, she had the same big blue eyes, long wavy blonde hair and easy smile. The pub fell silent for a second as people noted the new arrival, before conversations began again. Lucy started circulating and introducing her mother to Rob and the colonel, before moving on to the rest of the pub. Sadie greeted each new acquaintance with a kiss and an exclamation of delight, but Jo soon noticed that she barely bothered to remember any names and instead called everyone 'darling'. Lucy finally left her chatting to an enthralled Reverend Davenport and joined Jo at the bar.

"G&T please, Jack. And make it a large one," she said exhaling loudly.

Jo gave her a questioning look.

"We called into the dower house on our way here," Lucy explained. "I thought I should introduce Caroline to Sadie before everyone else met her."

"I bet you could have sold tickets," replied Jo with a wry

smile. She might only have been in Hartwell for a few months, but she had the measure of Lucy's mother-in-law and she was positive Caroline would not take kindly to Freddie's glamorous other granny taking up residence in Hartwell Hall.

"It was like two alley cats facing off." Lucy cringed. "Honestly, I thought at any minute they'd start hissing and clawing at each other."

"No offence to your mum, but I think my money would be on Caroline." Jo laughed, then stopped when she saw the door open and Rachel appeared with a very subdued and pale Becky. Again there was a lull in the conversation.

Lucy immediately jumped down from her stool and went to greet the two sisters. Jo watched her make a big show of hugging first Becky and then Rachel.

"Birds of a feather flock together," she heard Nora mutter to her cronies. "Another one happy to be gadding about after her husband disappears. I bet there's more going on there than meets the eye."

Jo was very tempted to put the old bag straight, but Lucy called over to her, "We're going to sit in the window table. Are you joining us?"

"I'll bring the drinks," Jo replied. She turned to Jack. "What does Becky drink?"

"Prosecco usually."

Jo pulled a face. She wasn't a fan of the fizzy wine her friends seemed to like so much.

"Better give me a bottle and three glasses," she said.

"I'll grab you one from out of the fridge," said Jack as he disappeared into the side bar. While she waited, Jo turned her attention back to Lucy's mother, who had quickly extracted herself from Reverend Davenport and was now scanning the men in the room with an expert eye. Then she watched as Sadie sidled over to Colonel Marsden and smiled up at him coquettishly. The colonel had turned a deep shade of red and was about to offer her a drink, when Lucy hurried over and dragged her away to meet Rachel and Becky.

"Better make it four glasses," Jo called over to Jack.

A little while later, she and Rachel were left alone with Sadie. Lucy had gone to the bar for another bottle of prosecco and Becky had left after only ten minutes, complaining of a headache.

"How are you finding Hartwell?" asked Rachel politely.

"Oh, it's absolutely gorgeous. The perfect English village. I wish I'd discovered it sooner," trilled Sadie.

"Why didn't you? Visit sooner I mean?" asked Jo.

Rachel gave her a wary look, but Sadie didn't flinch.

"My life in South Africa is so busy. I have so many commitments: charity events, parties. It's quite exhausting. Naturally, as soon as I read about Rupert disappearing, I was desperate to be with poor Lucy, but there were months of terrible travel restrictions. They were lifted just as I heard about the awful stalking episode. I dropped everything to be here by my daughter's side."

Sadie gave Jo a dazzling smile, but she only nodded in response. She wasn't convinced by her doting mother act. Something didn't add up.

"I'm sure Lucy appreciates you being here," said Rachel politely.

Sadie patted her on the arm. "What a lovely thing to say,

darling. Now if you'll both excuse me I must go and powder my nose."

Sadie stood up, but instead of heading to the ladies' she slinked back over to the snug and the unsuspecting colonel.

"You do know she's not under arrest, don't you?" hissed Rachel.

"What do you mean?"

"You are treating Lucy's mother like she's an arch-criminal."

"Don't exaggerate. I was civil. I only wondered why she's turned up now after all this time."

"Like she said, she heard her only daughter had lost her husband and been the victim of a stalker."

"You believe that?"

Rachel picked up her glass and gave a deep sigh. "It doesn't matter if I do or not if Lucy is happy to have her here. This is the first time in ages she's had a night out with us." She glanced across to where Lucy was laughing at one of Jack's jokes. "And she hasn't stopped smiling since she arrived here." Rachel took a sip of her drink and shook her head. "I'm not saying I believe every word Sadie says, but when it comes to Lucy, I've decided it's probably better if I take a step back."

"I thought you'd moved on?"

"I have."

"And Lucy's still your friend, isn't she?"

"Of course she is and I'd do anything to help her, but with families things aren't always as black and white as you seem to think. I'm sure there are plenty of people here who would say I shouldn't trust Becky after what happened with

Max, but she's my sister and I love her, even if I don't always like her. Perhaps you are right and there is more to Sadie being here than meets the eye, but if Lucy sees this as a chance to finally have a relationship with her mother, I don't think she'll thank you if you start rocking the boat."

"All right, all right. I'll keep my mouth shut," muttered Jo quietly as Lucy returned to the table.

By last orders, the place was almost empty. Lucy and Rachel had left an hour earlier, but Jo had remained behind chatting to Jack and Rob. Now only Sadie and the colonel remained in the snug. Jack helped escort the two of them, who were both a little unsteady on their feet, to the door while Jo knocked back the last of her beer.

"It's a good thing the colonel lives within staggering distance," Jack said as he bolted the door behind them. "Have you got time for another one and a game of snooker?"

"Sure, if you don't mind losing again," replied Jo cheerfully. She'd lost count of the nights they'd spent playing snooker or darts, often into the early hours, chatting and drinking.

"My luck's got to change soon," he said as she followed him through to the games room at the back of the pub.

"I keep telling you it's skill not luck." She laughed while he racked up the balls.

Less than twenty minutes later, she'd cleared the table.

"You could at least pretend to give me a chance," grumbled Jack. "Loser gets the drinks," he said handing over a bottle of beer. Jo put down her cue and took a sip of beer. Jack rested against the table with an expression on his face she couldn't read.

"Are you okay?" he asked finally.

"Yes. Why wouldn't I be?"

Jack shrugged and looked a little embarrassed. "I know it's not quite the same, but I thought Lucy's mum turning up might have got you thinking about your family."

Jo rolled her eyes. "I keep telling you, I'm not interested in finding my parents. Yes, it's weird that my necklace comes from this village, but it doesn't mean I belong here or anything."

"Okay, okay," he said holding up his hands in mock surrender. "I only wanted to check you weren't upset."

She felt a pang of guilt. She loved these nights with Jack. They would put the world to rights, and he made her laugh more than anyone she'd ever met, but she knew he wanted more. She'd tried to explain that she wasn't looking for a relationship and all she really wanted was to get back to London, but it was clear he still hoped she might change her mind. Maybe she wasn't being fair. She put down her beer and pulled on her coat.

"I'm fine. Thanks for the game, but I think I'll call it a night. I'm knackered."

"I think you're just worried I'll win the next game," said Jack.

Jo laughed and shook her head. "Yep, that's definitely it."

THE NEXT DAY was a Saturday. Even after her morning run, Jo was still feeling a little hungover from the night before.

She was probably still over the limit and didn't want to risk driving to the supermarket in Thirsk, but she was in desperate need of coffee and toast. There was nothing for it—she would have to brave Nora.

As she approached the village shop, she spotted Sadie leaving. She was wearing huge black sunglasses, but she wasn't carrying anything. The flimsy floaty dress she was wearing certainly wasn't the type to have handy pockets. Jo watched her for a second before crossing the road and heading through the jangling door herself.

"Cheeky madam!" exclaimed Nora as soon as she stepped inside.

"I've literally just walked in," protested Jo indignantly.

"Not you," replied Nora with a dismissive wave of her hand. "Lady Muck!"

Jo assumed she meant Sadie but decided it was safer not to ask for confirmation and quietly began to fill her basket. Nora, however, was quite happy to continue her rant without encouragement.

"And I don't care how posh she sounds; I know her type. All fur coat and no knickers. No wonder her daughter is such a dizzy thing with her as a role model."

Jo silently placed her basket on the counter.

"Came in here wanting cigarettes and vodka with no cash to pay for it," continued Nora as she rang the few items through the till. "I told her we don't offer credit."

Jo wordlessly tapped her debit card against the PDQ machine and collected her goods.

"We're not a charity," Nora called after her.

"HAVE YOU GOT a minute?" Meera's head appeared over the garden wall.

Jo, who had been sunbathing, looked up from her laptop. "Sure, come over," she replied.

A second later, Meera came through the little wooden gate Ben had installed. Unlike Jo, climbing over walls wasn't really her thing. Baking, however, was and she came bearing a plate of chocolate muffins.

"I made these for Krish to take to Freddie's, but there were some left over."

"Is he up at the Hall now?"

"Yes, I thought it was for the best and Lucy said she didn't mind. I missed a call from Dev earlier. He said he needed to talk to me and would call back."

Jo looked up with interest. "Do you think Darren has contacted him again?"

"Maybe." She sighed sitting down on the old bench next to Jo. "I don't know whether I want him to or not. What are you doing?"

"Googling Sadie," replied Jo, helping herself to a muffin.

"Why?"

Jo shrugged with her mouth half full. "I don't buy her story of suddenly feeling all maternal, when she read about Lucy in the papers."

"You can be very suspicious sometimes, Jo," tutted Meera.

"Duh! That is pretty much my job, Meera. I'm only looking out for Lucy. Last night after Rachel and Lucy left the pub, she hung around. She was flirting with anything in trousers and running up a tab; she told Jack Lucy would pay. That's not exactly bonding with her daughter and only grandson." Jo turned her attention back to the screen. "Wow, she was a real party girl back in the day!"

Meera peered over her shoulder. "Oh my goodness! She's completely naked in that one!" She gasped, pointing to a picture of a pouting Sadie wearing nothing more than a strategically placed feather boa.

Jo ignored her as she continued to scroll through all the various news articles and photos. She clicked on a recent picture of Sadie on the arm of a handsome, silver-haired man with a deep mahogany tan.

"This must be her latest boyfriend. Louis Van der Stamp."

"Really? I know him. He played Heathcliff in an old adaptation of *Wuthering Heights*. His English accent wasn't very good though," mused Meera, while Jo typed in the actor's name.

The first image that appeared on the screen was of the same handsome man standing on a red carpet with his arm wrapped firmly around the tiny waist of an attractive blonde, who looked about twenty years old. Jo quickly scanned through the accompanying article.

"I knew it!" she declared. "Sadie has been traded in for a younger model. It says here, Louis moved his new girlfriend into his palatial home overlooking Bantry Bay."

"Poor Sadie!" said Meera. "But it doesn't necessarily mean she's using Lucy. Perhaps the break-up of her relationship made her re-evaluate her life," she suggested hopefully.

"You aren't going to say anything to Lucy, are you?"

"Don't you think I should?" asked Jo, who generally worked on honesty being the best policy.

Meera gave a firm shake of her head. "No. Families can be complicated. Believe me, I know that better than most. I don't think Lucy will thank you if you do or say anything that makes Sadie leave."

"If you say so, but I think we should both keep an eye on her. Lucy's had a hell of a year and we both know she isn't the best judge of character."

Jo sighed as she closed the laptop. Meera was echoing what Rachel had said. Whatever Jack might think about her need to find her family, she was relieved she didn't have to deal with these sorts of problems herself. She was about to reach for another muffin when Meera's phone began to ring.

"It's Dev," she said. "I'll make it a FaceTime call, so we can both speak to him."

Jo leaned in to see the screen, as Meera answered.

"Hello, Dev! I'm here with Jo. Is there any news?"

Dev frowned back at them both. He looked much healthier than when Jo had last seen him.

"Yes, Darren called last night. He repeated his demands, but this time he lowered the amount he's asking for to one thousand pounds."

"He's getting desperate," murmured Jo.

"What did you say?" asked Meera.

"I told him what we agreed. That I would meet him with the money. He's going to call again with the time and place."

"Okay," replied Meera. Jo could tell she was struggling to remain calm. "So you'll call us again when it's all arranged so Jo can be there?"

"Actually, I'm not sure," said Dev cautiously.

"What do you mean?" asked Meera sounding wary.

"I'm not sure I should be the one to hand the money over. What if something goes wrong? I have to think of my position. There could be repercussions. I am a criminal barrister after all. It wouldn't do for my name to be connected to a blackmailer."

"Even if it meant protecting your son?" asked Meera. She sounded incredulous and Jo didn't blame her. What sort of a father was he?

Dev ignored his wife and turned to address Jo. "We know Darren is a drug dealer. Couldn't I give you the details of the meeting and you arrest him on suspicion of supplying? If you find drugs on him or in his car, you could charge him, and you wouldn't even need to mention me."

Jo glowered at the screen. He was certainly thinking like a lawyer now.

"There's no guarantee we'd find anything, and we'd still need someone to hand the money over," she replied.

"What if one of your colleagues took my place?"

Jo shook her head. "It's not that easy."

"Why not? Surely you'd have more chance of arresting him?" argued Dev.

"Put it this way, our station isn't the most diverse. There are only two Asian officers and one of them is female."

"What about the other one?" asked Meera.

Jo shook her head again. "He's only about five foot four and almost as wide as he is tall. He'd never pass for Dev in a million years."

"Well, you'll have to try and find someone. I'll supply you with the time and place, even the money if necessary, but it's simply too risky for me to be there." With that Dev disappeared from the screen.

"I don't believe him. Just when I think he can't be any more selfish, he surpasses himself." Meera sounded close to tears. Jo put her arm around her.

"Try not to get upset. We can't force him to be there. The main thing is, if Darren thinks he's getting the money there's no reason for him to come to Hartwell."

"But who are we going to get to do the handover?"

"I'll think of something," Jo assured her as she began to rack her brains for someone who could stand in for Dev.

"I wish Ben was here." Meera sighed.

"When is he back?"

"The end of the week, I think. The line hasn't been great whenever he's phoned."

Jo looked at her in surprise. Knowing how Ben felt about Meera and Krish she would have expected him to have headed home immediately.

"You have told him about all this, haven't you?" she asked as she rubbed her temples. A plan was beginning to form in her mind.

Meera shook her head. "No. I didn't want to bother him when he was away. I was worried he might not take me seriously. He always says I worry too much. Also, I didn't want him to think I was this helpless female. Krish is my son and I should be able to protect him myself. Why, do you think I should have?" she asked.

"Probably," sighed Jo, "but don't worry about that now. Look, I've had an idea about how we catch Darren, but I'm not sure you're going to like it."

CHAPTER TEN

Lucy couldn't sleep. The glowing red numbers on her bedside clock told her it was quarter past two in the morning. How many nights had she lain in the darkness, owls screeching outside as she watching the minutes tick by? Everyone who knew her thought of her as this happy, outgoing, bubbly blonde, but nobody knew how many things preyed on her mind. It must have been years since she'd had a decent night's sleep.

At first, she'd worried about Rupert. Worried about what he was doing when he disappeared to London, then she worried about what sort of mood he would be in when he came home. After that terrible night when she'd hit him, she'd worried if he would ever come back again at all.

More recently, she'd tossed and turned about the thought of Guy returning to Hartwell or having to face him in court. That morning she'd heard the case was due to be heard in November, as if that cold, grey, damp month wasn't miserable enough.

Then there was the constant worry of running the estate. It felt like she was taking one step forward, but two steps back. The success of the weddings and filming contracts was in danger of being cancelled out by the inheritance tax. Now there was this business with Max stealing from them. She'd almost been sick when she realised how much he'd stolen. No wonder the estate was in such a mess. What he'd done to her was nothing compared to what he'd done to poor Mary and Becky though.

She turned her head. The little red lights told her it was now three o'clock. It would be light before she knew it. She gave her pillow a thump and rolled on to her side. On top of everything else, there was now her mother. Jack had brought a very tipsy Sadie home at midnight, after she'd tried unsuccessfully to convince him to hold a lock-in for her and a few of the bemused young farmers she'd befriended. Lucy had finally managed to get her into bed, leaving a bottle of water and some Alka-Seltzer for her and, to be safe, a bucket in case she couldn't make it to the bathroom in time.

When Sadie had first turned up on her doorstep, Lucy had hoped they might actually be able to have the mother-daughter relationship she'd always longed for, but she hadn't bargained for playing the role of the mother herself. Having Sadie staying with her was like looking after a particularly difficult teenager. She never went to bed before one o'clock in the morning and didn't surface until midday. She left a trail of dirty cups, glasses and clothes throughout the house and Lucy was constantly having to replenish the bottles of gin and vodka she kept on the drinks table in the library. What upset her most was that she seemed far more interested in what the film crew were doing than getting to know Freddie.

Lucy wasn't the only one whose routine had been disrupted by her mother's arrival. Only that morning she'd walked into the kitchen and found Joan sewing a button on to one of Sadie's miniskirts, but before she could ask her about it, Bill had appeared in the doorway laden down with armfuls of laundry he was bringing back from the dry-cleaner's. One look at the brightly coloured silky fabric inside told her it all belonged to her mother.

"What are you both doing?" she'd asked. "Did Sadie ask you to pick up her laundry?"

"We don't mind helping out, Lady H. She is your mother after all," replied Bill as he carefully hung the garments on the coat hook on the back of the door, before politely raising his cap and heading outside again.

"Besides," added Joan after her husband had gone, "the first time she tried turning on the washing machine, she nearly flooded the place. Between you and me, I don't think she's very domesticated."

"I just don't want her taking advantage of you," replied Lucy as she filled the kettle and began nibbling one of Joan's shortbread biscuits while she waited for it to boil. The older lady watched her as she expertly broke off the thread with her teeth.

"I hope that isn't your breakfast, love. You need to eat properly. You've been so busy dashing around with all these new bookings recently, but you need to remember to take care of yourself too."

"Okay, okay, I'll have a banana as well. Happy now?" asked Lucy with a smile as she poured the hot water into the teapot and carried it over to the table.

"How about I make a nice quiche and salad for lunch?" suggested Joan.

"That sounds lovely," said Lucy, "but I'll probably only have time for a quick sandwich. The advertising people who took the photos for that knitwear brand want to come and take another look around the estate. I said I'd help them find locations for a shoot they want to do for a new four-wheel-drive car, then the wedding planner is coming over to confirm the position of the marquee for this weekend's wedding."

"Goodness! It all seems to be going really well and it's all down to you. Let's hope with Max no longer here, the estate should go from strength to strength."

Joan and Bill had been shocked when they'd heard what the estate manager had been up to.

"I do hope so," said Lucy taking a sip of tea. "Even after the death duties, I might still be able to get the roof fixed before winter. Imagine, not having to dash around with buckets as soon as it starts to rain. Rob is going to bring a roofing contractor he knows over to give me a quote."

"That's nice of him. The two of you do seem to be spending a lot of time together," said Joan with a knowing smile. At that moment, the door opened, and a yawning Sadie wandered in wearing a red silk kimono.

"Morning, Mum," said Lucy standing up and going over to the kettle. "Would you like a cup of tea?"

"I'm not really a fan of tea, darling. It always seemed like an old lady's drink to me. I'd kill for a decent espresso though," Sadie declared dramatically, as she collapsed on to the chair Lucy had just vacated.

"Sorry, we've only got instant," replied Lucy as she scooped a couple of large spoonfuls of coffee powder into a mug. "By the way, Bill has picked up your dry-cleaning this morning."

"Oh, I wish I'd known—I could have asked him to grab a Starbucks too." Sadie sighed, and then seeming to notice Joan for the first time. "Joan sweetie, when you've finished that would you mind giving my bathroom a quick tidy? The place looks like a bomb's hit it."

"Of course," replied Joan politely, standing up and holding out the fixed skirt to Sadie.

"Oh, and leave that on my bed too, will you?"

Joan nodded wordlessly, before disappearing out of the door.

"Mother," hissed Lucy when she'd gone, "you could at least say thank you."

"Don't be silly, darling. You don't need to thank servants."

Lucy bristled. "Joan and Bill aren't servants. They have been like family to me," she explained placing the steaming mug down on the table.

Sadie pulled a face as she took a sip of her coffee. "But you do pay them. And they do live rent-free on the estate."

"Well yes, but their accommodation comes with their jobs."

"And I'm sure they do those jobs competently enough, but I've always thought it's a good idea to maintain a little distance when it comes to staff. Making them cups of tea probably isn't such a good idea, darling. I'd hate for them to take advantage of you." She reached across the table and gave Lucy's hand a squeeze. "I'm sure you must have been lonely these last few months, but you've got me now. I'm your real family."

"Did you have a nice time last night?" asked Lucy. "I didn't hear you come in." She felt uncomfortable discussing Joan and Bill like this.

"I only popped down to the White Hart for a few drinks. It's such a fun crowd down there. The colonel invited me for a nightcap after last orders. He really is a charming man. Has he been a widower long?"

"A few years," replied Lucy cautiously. Sadie gave her a sidelong glance.

"That handsome builder of yours was in the pub too. Did you know he wears a Rolex? I suppose it must be fake or you're paying him far too much."

"He's not my builder," protested Lucy. "He just got some of his team to help me tidy the place up a bit, and I doubt anyone made enough here to buy an egg timer, let alone a Rolex, but why shouldn't he have a nice watch? He works really hard. I think he converted lots of warehouses or factories or something in Leeds."

"Is that so? Handsome, single and rich. My three favourite words. He sounds too good to be true. No skeletons in his closet?"

Lucy felt herself flush. "Not really," she stammered. "I mean, he has been to prison, but he was only trying to protect someone close to him."

"So that doesn't bother you at all, darling?"

Lucy opened her mouth to reply, but at that moment her phone, which she'd left on the table, began to ring. Both women automatically looked at the screen. Rob's name was flashing.

"Speak of the devil!" exclaimed Sadie with a sly smile.

Feeling embarrassed, Lucy snatched it up and hurried through into the hall to answer it. When she returned, Sadie was still sitting at the kitchen table flicking through one of the folders from the accountants. She put it down and shook her head when she saw Lucy.

"Honestly, darling. All those figures look like an utter nightmare. How do you manage to understand them?"

"I don't. At least not very well," admitted Lucy.

"Oh dear! You must take after me. I was always useless at maths."

"That's what Rob was ringing about. He's going to call round later and check some figures I've been working on."

"How kind. Although I've yet to meet a man who does a good deed without wanting something in return."

"Rob isn't like that," Lucy insisted.

Sadie arched an eyebrow. "Then he must be the exception to the rule. It's strange. I rather got the feeling when I saw the saw the two of you together that he wanted to be more than friends."

"Well maybe he does," said Lucy feeling herself blush again under Sadie's scrutiny and remembering her conversation with Rob up on the moors, "and he is terribly attractive, but I don't want to rush into another relationship."

"I think that's very wise, darling. You have been through such a lot. You don't want to be pushed into anything. Much better to keep men at arm's length for a while, even one as gorgeous as Rob."

"You really think so? I mean he is a nice guy, and he gets on well with Freddie."

"I'm sure both those things are true, but take it from me, it's a much better idea to wait until you are totally sure." She paused. "And if in the meantime Rob finds someone else, he clearly isn't the man for you."

Lucy nodded. As tempting as Rob was, her life was far too messy for any more complications. "You're probably right. Thanks."

"No need to thank me, darling. What are mothers for if not to give advice?"

Lucy smiled and gave her mother a quick peck on the cheek, before dashing outside to check on the film crew and wait for the advertising people to arrive.

It was half past one when she waved the wedding planner off. Their meeting had taken longer than expected and now she only had half an hour to prepare before Caroline and the other members of the estate's board of directors were due to arrive. Lucy had arranged the meeting so she could tell them about Max, and she was dreading it. Caroline was bound to blame her. She still hadn't told her mother-in-law about not being able to hold the village fete at Hartwell Hall yet either, but that would have to wait. There was only so much of Caroline's disapproval she could take in one day. She quickly showered and changed into a navy suit that she hoped made her look more serious and business-like than she felt.

At precisely two o'clock Lucy heard Caroline's Volvo chugging up the drive, followed by her mother-in-law complaining loudly that a cameraman's van was parked in front of the entrance. Lucy collected several folders from her office and hurried downstairs as quickly as she could.

"Hello, Caroline," she called out. Her mother-in-law

gave her a brief wave of acknowledgement as she went through into the dining room, glaring frostily at Sadie who was sprawled on a chaise longue reading an old copy of *Tatler*. She unfolded herself as Lucy came down the stairs.

"Would you like me to sit in, darling? You know for moral support?" asked Sadie as she waved over Lucy's shoulder at the beaming colonel who had just arrived.

"No thanks, Mum. Maybe you could do something with Freddie. Go for a walk perhaps. It would be nice for him to be out of the house with all this going on," she suggested.

"Maybe later, darling. It looks like rain, don't you think?" replied Sadie as she drifted off into the library where sun was streaming in through the French windows, and she poured herself the first gin and tonic of the day. Following the colonel and Caroline were the other two board members: Mr Bradbury, the accountant, and Mr Harrowell, the estate's solicitor. Feeling slightly queasy, Lucy went to join them all in the dining room.

"So, Lucinda," began Caroline from her position at the head of the table, "perhaps you could enlighten us as to why you have called this extra ordinary meeting."

"It's not good news, I'm afraid," Lucy began hesitantly, handing them each a folder. She had practised what she wanted to say in her head hundreds of times, but now the words seemed to have disappeared; her mind had gone totally blank. "Max has gone," she blurted out. Four faces frowned back at her.

"What do you mean gone? Has he given notice? Do we need to advertise for a new agent?" asked the colonel.

Lucy shook her head. "No. He's disappeared. Nobody

seems to know where he is. The police think he might be abroad."

"The police?" queried Caroline, raising an eyebrow.

"Yes, you see he's been stealing from the estate," Lucy began to explain.

"Really, Lucinda, how could you let such a thing happen?!" exclaimed Caroline.

"How much did he get away with?" asked Mr Bradbury, before Lucy could reply.

"I've collated all the figures and put them in the folders in front of you," replied Lucy watching as the accountant opened his folder and turned pale as he read through the list.

"Good heavens," muttered the colonel, "what on earth did he do with it all?"

"Spent it," replied Lucy, "on holidays, expensive restaurants, that sort of thing."

Caroline gave the accountant a withering look. "How did you miss this, Bradbury?" she snapped.

"We only audit the accounts once a year. Most of these fraudulent transactions occurred in the last nine months," the account stammered, turning bright red.

"Don't worry, old boy," the colonel reassured him. "Not your fault. Or yours, Lucinda. Even MI5 discovered the odd rogue agent in their ranks. It can't be helped. Rupert, Caroline and I interviewed Max. He seemed like a decent enough chap. Decent references. Put roots down in the village. Married a local girl. I thought he was one of us. It goes to show you can never tell."

Lucy smiled gratefully at him, while Caroline turned impatiently to the solicitor.

"Where do we stand legally? Can we pursue him through the courts in his absence?"

While Harrowell seemed to be pondering his reply, Lucy answered instead.

"What would be the point? Max doesn't have any assets. He was up to his ears in debt," said Lucy. She had never warmed to Becky, but she was Rachel's sister, and she was determined not to make things worse for her. "I don't think we should pursue it. We should simply be thankful we found out what was going on when we did."

Caroline stared at her incredulously. "Are you quite mad? What sort of a message does it send out if we allow ourselves to be robbed and cheated and do nothing about it? He deserves to be punished," argued Caroline.

"But what would be the point?" repeated Lucy. "I've spoken to Rachel who's seen his bank statements. Any money he took, he's spent. We don't have any hope of getting it back. The only people we would hurt are his wife and daughter. They are victims too in a way."

Caroline gave a snort of derision.

"And another thing," continued Lucy, then paused, hoping she had picked the right time to play her trump card, "I don't think the estate can afford any more bad publicity. The events business seems to be going well. I've prepared a forecast of what I think the hall should earn for the rest of the year through weddings and filming contracts." She quickly stood up and handed the other directors the printout she had prepared. "Why do anything to risk it by attracting more negative publicity?"

"These figures certainly look encouraging, Lucinda. Well

done you," said the colonel, beaming across the table at her. "I had no idea weddings could be so lucrative."

"We've got bookings coming for next year already, Colonel," she explained, sensing she'd won the solicitor and account round too, "but brides can be superstitious. We've weathered the unpleasant press attention about Rupert and the business with Guy, but we don't want anyone to start thinking this place is unlucky."

"Quite," seconded Harrowell.

The colonel glanced around the table. "So are we all in agreement? We don't pursue a legal case against Max?"

"Agreed," murmured the accountant and solicitor. They all turned to Caroline.

"Agreed," she said reluctantly, "but if he returns to Hartwell, I reserve the right to reverse this decision."

The others nodded. They all knew life was much easier if Caroline felt she had got her own way. As the three men left the room, Caroline took her time to collect her belongings. When the two of them were alone, she fixed Lucy with her piercing stare.

"Do I take it Max was also responsible for what's been happening to poor Mary?" she asked in an unusually low voice.

"Yes. He's been gaslighting her."

"What an odd expression and what a very unpleasant man he turned out to be."

"It's better for everyone that he's gone."

Caroline pursed her lips. "Let's hope he doesn't turn up again like the proverbial bad penny."

CHAPTER ELEVEN

MEERA PICKED UP the phone then immediately put it down again. She'd done the same thing three times now, still unsure what she would say. Thanks to Jo they had a clear, concise plan to deal with Darren, but it was up to Meera to put the first part of it into action. Before she could change her mind again, she quickly pressed the number that was programmed into her speed dial list, but that she hardly ever called. It rang six times before her brother finally answered.

"Yo! Who is it?"

Meera rolled her eyes. Clearly Nish hadn't thought it worth entering her number into his own phone and why couldn't he say 'hello' like a normal person?

"Nish, it's me."

"What do you want?" he replied. As charming as ever, thought Meera. He hadn't even bothered to turn down the Bhangra music blaring in the background. She could barely hear him.

"I need your help," she replied trying to keep her tone even.

"Yeh right, since when?" he snorted.

She took a deep breath.

"Since now. Please, Nish, I mean it."

The music fell silent.

"What's up? Is it Krish? Is he ill?" Her brother's voice sounded serious all of a sudden.

"No, Krish is fine. It's Dev."

"I thought he was in India seeing his family."

"No, he's back now."

"And?"

Meera was about to reply, but she really didn't know how to start. "Actually, it's a bit complicated to explain over the phone. Could you come over?"

There was a pause at the other end of the line and Meera was sure he was about to tell her to get lost or that he was too busy.

A wave of relief washed over her when she heard him say, "Okay. I'll be with you in an hour."

True to his word, fifty minutes later, Meera heard the sound of a car engine roaring down the lane and coming to an abrupt screeching halt outside her cottage.

"What's all this about?" he asked after he'd turned down her offer of tea and flopped down on her sofa.

"Dev is being blackmailed," began Meera.

Nish snorted in disbelief. "What? Why?"

Meera took a deep breath. "Because he's gay."

Nish leaned back against the sofa and stared at her. "You're kidding me, right?"

"It really isn't the sort of thing I would kid about, Nish."

"You sure?"

Meera didn't even bother to answer this time—she just glared back at her brother.

"How long have you known?" he asked.

"Since our wedding night."

"What about Krish? Is he Dev's?"

"Yes, of course he is!" she snapped.

"So is Dev like bi or something?"

"Nish, I really don't want to discuss Dev's sexuality. All you need to know is that he's been trying to keep it secret and now someone is blackmailing him."

"Poor guy!" muttered Nish, surprising Meera a little. She'd never really thought of her brother as being particularly sympathetic.

"I thought you didn't like him. You always said he was too good to be true."

"Yeh and it turns out I was right, doesn't it? Still, it can't have been easy growing up gay in a place where it was illegal. He must have been worried about upsetting his family."

"Yes, well, it gets worse. Dev tried to tell the blackmailer he wouldn't pay, and they started threatening Krish."

Nish leapt to his feet. "Bastards!" he cursed. "Are they serious?"

"I think so. The person who is blackmailing him is a drug dealer from Leeds, who has been seen dealing close to here. We think he also visited Krish's school."

"Then you should stop messing about and go straight to the police," said Nish firmly.

"I have done. I told Jo and she came up with a plan. Please stop pacing up and down and I'll tell you."

"That bolshie neighbour of yours?"

"She's not bolshie. Well only sometimes, but yes, she is my neighbour. She wants you to pretend to be Dev. When you go and hand the money over, she'll move in and arrest him. We are hoping she'll find drugs on him, because the evidence of blackmail is a bit flimsy."

Nish stopped pacing and gave her a sceptical look. "I don't understand. Why isn't Dev doing this?"

"He's doesn't want to be involved. He thinks it will damage his career. I'm afraid to say he's rather selfish."

Nish sat down again and shook his head. "You shouldn't be too hard on him, Meera."

Meera frowned. Of all the scenarios she'd imagined, Nish sticking up for Dev hadn't been one of them.

"Why not? This is all his fault for not being honest."

Nish snorted again. "Honest! Come on, you've met his father. He's not the understanding type. I'd probably keep quiet if he was my dad too. Besides, you can't really talk about being honest."

"What do you mean?"

"You've been married to Dev for ten years and only now you're telling me he's gay. And you are only telling me because you have to. All those lies about him working away because he had a big case or whatever, making excuses when he didn't turn up to family events. You haven't been honest with Mum and Dad, and you haven't been honest with me."

"I was protecting Dev. It wasn't my secret to tell," protested Meera. Her brother's words had stung.

"Really? Or did you not want everyone to know the truth? Little Miss Perfect's life wasn't so perfect after all."

"That's not fair!"

"Isn't it? All those family meals when Mum and Dad gave me a hard time about getting a job or settling down:

'Why can't you be more like your sister, Nish?' 'Why can't you get married?' You never once stepped in and said, 'Actually my marriage isn't so great.' You know it hasn't always been easy being your brother. Always being compared to Meera, who always does the right thing and is such a good daughter, clever doctor and perfect mother."

The two of them glared at each other for a moment. Meera was the first to look away.

"If that's the way you feel, I guess I shouldn't have asked you to help."

"Don't be stupid. You know I'll help if someone is threatening you or Krish, but I wish you could have been honest with me before now."

"I'm sorry," said Meera quietly.

Nish sat staring at his feet, before finally looking up. "You really think this plan will work?"

"We think so. Shall I call Jo and ask her to come over?"

JO AND NISH had only met once before, when Jo had walked in on him yelling at his sister. The two of them surveyed each other warily from either side of her sitting room, reminding Meera of two tigers meeting in the wild, like on one of the natural history documentaries Krish watched.

"All right?" Jo greeted him with a brusque nod of the head.

"All right," replied Nish.

"I've outlined our plan to Nish," said Meera. "And he's willing to help."

"Great," replied Jo. "Dev has arranged to meet Darren, the guy blackmailing him, outside a wine bar in Harrogate. You just need to hand the money over and we'll move in. We're hoping to find evidence of blackmail on his phone, but there's also a good chance we'll get him for possession too. So, no heroics from you, okay?" she warned.

Nish scowled. "Why Harrogate, if he's from Leeds?" he asked.

"Three reasons," Jo began to explain. "Leeds is in West Yorkshire, so it's not as straightforward for me to make an arrest there. Also, Darren might feel more relaxed away from a city where the local police know him, put him off his guard a bit."

"We also got Dev to suggest Harrogate because we thought it might be suspicious if he didn't alter the plan Darren suggested a little bit," chimed in Meera. "It might have seemed like he was agreeing too readily. Also, Harrogate, with all its bistros and wine bars, is quite a Dev sort of place."

"It'll be dark when you meet. You and Dev are the same height and build. Darren only saw Dev once when he represented him in court and that was over two years ago, and he would have been wearing a wig and gown," continued Jo.

"Dev gave me the cash and some of his clothes, jewellery and scent for you to wear," added Meera. She didn't add that Dev had been more than willing to drop everything off, then hurry back across the Pennines and let everyone else do his dirty work.

"Okay you've convinced me," said Nish. "When do we

do it?"

The two women exchanged a look.

"Tonight," replied Meera tentatively. "Sorry. I know it's very short notice."

Dev rolled his eyes. "You can say that again. What would you have done if I'd said 'no'?"

"I sort of hoped you wouldn't," replied Meera with a weak smile.

MEERA SAT NERVOUSLY tapping her fingers against the steering wheel as they waited for Jo's phone call. They had driven through a heavy rainstorm on the way and the fashionable spa town of Harrogate was unusually quiet for a summer's evening. Nish sat next to her in the passenger seat. He was dressed in one of Dev's pinstriped suits and trench coat with the collar turned up and after much complaining he'd allowed Meera to style his hair the way Dev wore his. She'd even sprayed him with some of the aftershave Dev wore.

"You don't think you're getting a bit carried away, do you?" he'd grumbled.

"I thought it would help you get into character," she'd replied. "And Darren might remember it. Your sense of smell is closely linked to your memory and we want to do as much as we can to make him think you are Dev."

Nish sighed heavily and rolled his eyes. Meera had parked her car in an unlit street of stone terraced houses. At the top of the street, on the corner, they could see the wine bar where the exchange was due to take place. She turned on the radio. Another of the Proms concerts from London was being broadcast. After a few minutes, Nish reached over and changed the channel.

"What are you doing?" protested Meera.

"Putting something decent on. That was doing my head in."

"Well, I found it very soothing. It's Vivaldi."

"I know. Mum and Dad made me learn the violin until I was sixteen, remember. I'm not completely uncultured."

"I never said you were, and I think it's a shame you didn't continue with the violin."

Their bickering was interrupted by the shrill ring of Meera's phone. They both looked down at the screen. Jo's name flashed back at them. Nish put his hand out, but Meera swatted it away and picked it up herself.

"Meera, it's me," she said. "Darren has just stepped outside."

"Wish me luck," said Nish, opening the car door.

"Good luck! And remember to keep your head tilted down," Meera hissed after him.

Her heart was pounding as she watched her brother walk down the street. There was a streetlight outside the entrance to the wine bar and she could make out the man with the shaved head smoking a cigarette. She held her breath as Nish approached him. A few seconds later, she saw him hand over the envelope. Then everything happened very quickly. There was a shout and Jo appeared. Darren shoved Nish out the way and came sprinting down the street. Nish and Jo started to chase after him, but two cars whizzing by stopped them getting across the road.

Meera began to panic. Darren was heading straight towards her. He was going to get away. He was getting closer. There was only one thing she could do. She put her hand on the door handle, waited until he was almost level, then pushed it open with all her strength. The impact knocked Darren off his feet and sent him sprawling across the pavement. Meera stepped out without any idea of what to do next, but a second later Jo and Nish dashed across the street and came running towards her.

"Are you okay?" asked Nish breathlessly as he reached her. Meera nodded although she could feel herself trembling. Jo had dropped to her knees and was clapping handcuffs on to the groaning Darren whilst she read him his rights. She put her hand in his coat pocket and pulled out his phone and a small pack of round white tablets.

"Bingo," she said, smiling up at Meera. "This should be enough to charge him." She turned and shouted to a chubby young man who was lumbering down the street towards them, "Dawson, bring the car round!"

MEERA WAS SHAKING so much, Nish insisted on driving the two of them back to Hartwell while Jo and her partner took Darren to the police station.

"That was excellent," said Nish, who couldn't stop himself grinning. "I just wish I'd got to punch the bastard."

"Then Jo would have needed to arrest you for assault," tutted Meera.

"Relax. I was only joking," he muttered. "I thought you'd be happy it's all over."

"I am and I'm very grateful to you, but it's been a very stressful few days."

Nish gave her a sidelong glance. "Are you going to be okay? Do you want me to stay over? Should I take you to Mum and Dad's?"

Meera shook her head. "Thank you, but no. I'll be fine. I just want to go home."

"They would want to know about this and about you and Dev."

Meera remained silent. Nish gestured to the mobile phone resting on her lap. She'd forgotten the screen saver was a photo of her, Ben and Krish by a loch in Scotland.

"Who's he?" her brother asked.

"His name is Ben. Krish and I went on holiday to Scotland with him."

Nish shook his head and clicked his tongue impatiently. "Are you going to keep him a secret from Mum and Dad too? They are upset. They haven't heard from you in ages and Mum thinks you're avoiding her calls."

Meera felt a pang of guilt. He was right. For weeks she'd been fobbing her parents off with bright, but brief text messages.

"I know," she said quietly, "and I will tell them. I promise, but please don't say anything yet. I can't cope with any more drama right now."

AS SOON AS she arrived back at her cottage, she called Dev.

"Well?" he asked as soon as he answered.

"Darren is under arrest. Jo has his phone, and she also found some drugs on him, so she'll be able to charge him," she told him.

"That's wonderful news! Meera, how can I ever thank you?" said Dev. His voice sounded relaxed and Meera could perfectly imagine his handsome face smiling with relief.

"Divorce me," she said simply.

"What?"

"I mean it. It's up to you what you tell people, but I'm not living a lie anymore. Nish knows the truth and it's only a matter of time until I tell my parents."

There was silence at the end of the line and for a second she wondered if he'd hung up on her, but then she heard him sigh.

"I'll speak to a divorce lawyer I know tomorrow and set the wheels in motion. Okay?"

"Thank you," she said quietly. She put the phone down and waited. The familiar sense of panic began to rise within her as she knew it would. Breathing deeply several times, she closed her eyes and waited for it to subside. This was one decision she knew for sure she would not regret. It was a huge change, but a good one.

Chapter Twelve

"**I** DON'T UNDERSTAND. How can I not have any money at all?"

Rachel closed her eyes. Becky's whining was giving her a headache. She had spent the whole morning closing bank accounts, putting stops on credit cards and paying minimum amounts while an ashen-faced Becky sat opposite her at the farmhouse kitchen table.

"You don't have any money because you spent everything Max earned and a lot more. He borrowed on credit cards and didn't pay it back, which means you owe what you borrowed as well as the interest," Rachel explained patiently for what felt like the hundredth time. "Just be grateful Lucy isn't pursuing you through the courts for what he stole from her."

It turned out the bill Jo had found was just the tip of the iceberg. Rachel veered from wanting to wrap her arms around Becky and tell her everything would be okay, to wanting to shake her for being so stupid and never questioning her husband about how they were financing their extravagant lifestyle. At least now Rachel was convinced her sister had been completely ignorant of what Max was up to. Mary had agreed to pay off the most pressing debts that he had taken out in Becky's name, but there was still a frightening amount to get through.

Mary bustled back and forth cheerfully, making endless cups of tea for the three of them while Minty played outside in the old Wendy house that had once belonged to Rachel and Becky. Their mother was the only person who didn't seem too upset by Max's disappearance. Even when Rachel had come across a power of attorney that Max must have had drawn up, Mary had only shaken her head and tutted.

Rachel waved away the offer of another cup of tea. She needed a break. She left the house and walked through the farmyard gate towards her cottage, breathing in the fresh air. It was a glorious day and she had been cooped up long enough trying to sort out the mess Max had left behind. Becky and Minty had done as Mary suggested and moved back in with Mary. There was no way they would be able to afford the rent on the barn conversion now. This also meant Rachel could finally move back to her cottage. Mary no longer needed looking after and as sympathetic as she was to Becky's predicament, Rachel had her limits, and sharing a house with her sister was one of them.

She stopped and watched as two glossy bay mares from the local riding school clip-clopped by. Ideally, she would have liked to go up to her cousin Dan's farm on the moors where she stabled her old pony, Bailey. The two of them could have gone for a long ride, but there wasn't time now. She'd wasted a perfectly lovely day ploughing through statements. As she passed by the village shop the front door jangled open and Lucy stepped out laden down with two bags full of gin, vodka and wine.

"Bloody hell, Luce! I thought I was having a bad day. You've got enough there to sink a battleship."

"I'm restocking," replied Lucy, before lowering her voice. "It's my mother. She can drink like a fish."

"What about you? Have you got time for a quick one?" asked Rachel nodding in the direction of the White Hart.

"Always," agreed Lucy with a grin. "Just let me put all this in the car. I don't want Jack and Shirley thinking I'm trying to smuggle my own booze in."

When they entered the pub, there was nobody inside except for Jack and his mother. Shirley, whose hair today was a bright shade of orange, was sitting at one of the tables with her laptop open and a pile of papers by her side. Jack was taping a notice on to the window.

"I'll be with you in a second," he said, removing a roll of Sellotape from his mouth. "For some weird reason Chloe has decided that spending a gap year in India will be more interesting than staying here to dish up cottage pie and roast beef, so we're looking for a new waitress."

An idea suddenly occurred to Rachel. "Well, you can take that notice straight back down again. I've got the perfect person for you: Becky."

Jack and Shirley exchanged a look.

Rachel held up her hands. "Okay, okay, perfect might be pushing it, but she needs a job. She only lives across the road now, so she'll always be on time. She knows everyone in the village." Neither of them appeared to be convinced. "Look, just give her a chance, for me, please."

"Okay," agreed Jack. "Tell her to come over on Sunday at eleven. She can help out at lunchtime. We'll see how it goes. What can I get you both? We don't usually see you here this early."

"I'm escaping from the mess Max has left for a little while," explained Rachel.

"And she found me restocking my drinks cabinet, which seems to have become a full-time job since Sadie showed up. Thank God she spends most evenings here," said Lucy.

Shirley gave a small cough and peered at them over her glasses. "On the subject of your mum, Lucy—she's run up quite a tab over the last few nights. She said you had agreed to it. I wouldn't normally mention it, but I'm doing the end-of-month accounts—" she gestured to the papers next to her "—and well it's sending things out of kilter a bit."

Lucy flushed. It was clear to Rachel this was the first she'd heard about the arrangement.

"Oh yes, of course. Silly me I completely forgot," Lucy said producing a credit card from her back pocket and handing it apologetically to Jack. "Sorry, I should have called in earlier."

After watching Lucy wince when she saw the receipt, Rachel carried their drinks out to the beer garden. She didn't think either of them wanted to spend any more time around accounts. They found a seat in the shade.

Lucy raised her glass and gave a wry smile. "To families."

"Families," echoed Rachel. She took a long drink and sighed. "Look, I hate to add to your problems, but you are going to have to find new tenants for the barn. I'll get Becky to give you notice officially but there is no way she can afford to live there now."

"It's okay. I was expecting it. There's still no news about

Max, I take it?"

"No, it's like he's disappeared into thin air, along with all the money he nicked. It's good of you not to press charges."

"There's no need to thank me. I couldn't see what good it would do. We aren't going to get the money back. Becky doesn't need any more hassle and I for one can only handle one court case at a time."

"If Max was here, I'd wring his neck," muttered Rachel into her drink. They sat in silence for a few minutes, watching as Baxter chased a squirrel through the garden and along the garden fence.

"It's a shame you had to cut your holiday short. Were you having a good time?" asked Lucy.

"Wonderful! The weather, the history, the food—everything was perfect, but it feels like a million years since I was there."

"Maybe you'll get to go there again one day."

"Fingers crossed."

Jack suddenly appeared in the doorway. "There's someone here to see you, Rach," he shouted down to them then moved to one side. Behind him stood a woman with red curly hair. She smiled shyly and raised her hand in greeting. Rachel jumped to her feet.

"Sarah!" she gasped. "What are you doing here?"

Sarah began making her way towards them, dragging a large holdall behind her.

"Have you come straight here from South America?" asked Rachel, rushing to help.

"Yes," she replied, "well via Naples. I had planned to surprise you as you couldn't make it to Peru, but when I arrived at the hotel, they said you had already gone home. I only had a few days left in South America, so when I got your email saying you were going to Italy, I thought I'd join you," Sarah explained looking a little embarrassed.

Rachel's hand flew to her mouth as she suddenly remembered the cryptic message.

"Gosh," gasped Lucy, quickly standing up. "Well I'm sure the two of you have lots to catch up on. Bye, Rach. Nice to see you again, Sarah," she called over as she hurried away. She disappeared through the gate leaving the two women alone.

"Is Lucy the reason you had to dash home?" asked Sarah. There were dark circles beneath her soft brown eyes, but her freckled nose and full mouth were exactly as Rachel remembered. She blinked dumbly as she tried to take in what her arrival might mean before answering.

"Erm what? No. It had nothing to do with Lucy. It's my family," she said sitting back down again, not knowing where to start.

Sarah looked relieved. "It's okay if you don't want to talk to me about it."

Rachel shook her head. She still couldn't quite believe that Sarah had travelled all the way to Italy to surprise her or that she was standing in front of her now.

"No, it's not that, but it's really complicated. It might take a while."

Sarah flopped down in the seat recently vacated by Lucy and smiled. "Well, the sun is shining, and there's nowhere else I need to be. Why don't we order a bottle of wine and you can tell me all about it?"

Two hours and a bottle of red later, Rachel had filled Sarah in on everything that had happened since she'd left Sorrento.

"I can't believe anyone would do that to your mother," she said when Rachel had finished. "No wonder you flew home when you found out what was going on."

"If I'd known you were on your way I might have been tempted to stay," admitted Rachel.

Sarah reached out and stroked her cheek. "How are your mum and sister now?"

"Okay, I think. Becky is still a bit shell-shocked, but I think Mum is mainly relieved to know she isn't ill."

"So, if you were to spend the night away from the farmhouse, they'd be okay with that?"

Rachel caught her breath as Sarah took her hand and laced her fingers through hers.

"Actually, I've been thinking it might be time for me to return to the cottage."

"What are we waiting for?"

THE NEXT MORNING, Rachel woke early. Knowing that her kitchen cupboards were bare, she left Sarah sleeping, crept out of the cottage and dashed over to the farmhouse. Mary was already pottering around the kitchen.

"Hello, love. You're up early. I didn't hear you come in last night."

"I spent the night at the cottage. I thought I'd move back there."

Mary looked disappointed. "That's a shame. I've enjoyed having both my girls under one roof again."

"Sorry, Mum, but I think we both know if I stayed here, I might end up killing Becky. That reminds me."

Recalling her conversation with Jack, Rachel headed out of the kitchen and ran upstairs. Becky was still fast asleep in her old bedroom. Rachel prodded her awake.

"I've got you a job. The White Hart needs a waitress. You start on Sunday."

"But I don't know how to be a waitress. And what about Minty?"

"Mum will keep an eye on her," replied Rachel, trying to keep the exasperation out of her voice. "You need a job, and you aren't qualified to do anything else."

"I don't know, Rach. It feels too soon."

"Nonsense. It'll keep your mind off things. Besides you want to pay Mum back for all money she's spent bailing you out, don't you?"

"Yes, I suppose," replied Becky still sounding reluctant. "I'll think about it." She flopped back against the pillow covered in pink butterflies and pulled the duvet back over her head. Rachel shook her head as she headed back downstairs. There was no helping some people.

"Would you like a bacon sandwich, love?" asked her mother who was already brandishing a frying pan.

"Actually, I was going to ask if I can raid your pantry and take something back for breakfast."

"Does that mean you weren't alone last night?" asked Mary innocently.

Rachel rolled her eyes. "Are you seriously telling me that

Shirley wasn't straight on the phone to let you know that Sarah is back in the village?"

Mary chuckled. "Well yes, she might have mentioned it. I've made you a hamper up with some fresh bread, eggs, milk and some homemade jam." She pointed to a wicker basket sitting on the table.

Rachel planted a kiss on top of Mary's head. "Thanks, Mum. You're the best."

"I STILL CAN'T believe you went all the way to Naples," said Rachel, biting into a slice of toast. She'd woken a slightly jet-lagged Sarah up with breakfast in bed. Sarah threw her head back against the pillow and laughed her throaty laugh.

"I saw your Instagram post showing the hotel you were staying in, and I had it all planned how I was going to surprise you. I thought I could show you Pompeii—I studied the site when I was a student."

"And like an idiot, I didn't click when I got your message."

"I couldn't believe it when the receptionist told me you'd already gone."

"Let's make a promise that we'll go there together one day."

"Definitely. In the meantime, we can concentrate on our own archaeological tourist attraction right here."

"Seriously? In Hartwell?"

"Absolutely! I've been thinking about it a lot. York has museums dedicated to Roman and Viking settlements, but how many places tell us about the Celts and Druids? They are part of our heritage too. Hartwell could be the centre of Celtic England. I've applied for funding to continue exploring the site and the guy who owns it is happy to help."

"Rob Harrison," supplied Rachel.

"That's him. And with your local knowledge, there's nothing to stop us."

Sarah's eyes were sparkling with excitement. It was infectious. Rachel felt a tingle and for a second didn't recognise it. It had been a long time since she'd felt excited about anything, but the idea of the two of them creating something special in her home village had ignited a spark.

CHAPTER THIRTEEN

I T WAS EARLY evening. Jo had decided to go for a run straight after work. She didn't often exercise twice in one day, but the last couple of weeks had been the most stressful she'd known since arriving in North Yorkshire. She shook her head as the rap music blared in her ears and her feet pounded the cobbles. She'd never had friends before coming to Hartwell and so far, they were turning out to be exhausting. What with Rachel finding out what Max had been up to, him disappearing and the whole thing with Meera's husband being blackmailed by a drug dealer. On the plus side, she'd arrested Darren. Nicking a minor crook like him wasn't going to be enough to get her back to London, but it was one less lowlife out on the streets.

Pulling out her AirPods as she reached the church, she slowed her pace and followed the path that led through the graveyard. She paused to catch her breath and stretch by one of the wooden benches next to the grave of the young archaeologist. Apparently, Sarah was a bit of an expert on him. Jo had bumped into her and Rachel the other day. They had both looked totally loved up. Jo was pleased for Rachel. It was about time she had some good luck.

Jo took a sip of water and sat down on the bench. She

often came here when she needed to think. It was calm and peaceful, not creepy at all. The sun was shining brightly on the face of the church clock. It was a little after six. There was plenty of time to head home, get a shower, then maybe go to the pub. Shielding her eyes, she could see plenty of cars parked outside the White Hart already. It would be busy, but she was sure Jack would find room for her. He always held back a couple of tables for the locals. She shook her head. Get her, calling herself a local!

She was about to leave when she saw Reverend Davenport shuffling a little unsteadily towards her. He'd clearly enjoyed a very late lunch at the Hart himself. He smiled and lifted his hand in greeting when he saw her.

"Good afternoon, Sergeant Ormond. I don't often see you here at St Michael's."

"I've been for a run. I was just stopping to catch my breath," explained Jo.

"You won't be joining us for Evensong? You would be most welcome," he offered, peering at her over his steel-rimmed glasses.

Jo shook her head. "Thanks, but no, sorry. I don't really believe. You know, in God."

She didn't want to offend the old man, but she didn't see any point in pretending.

Reverend Davenport, however, simply smiled benignly and patted her on the shoulder. "Never mind, my dear. He believes in you. Always remember that."

Jo smiled to herself as she watched the old man totter towards the church. She downed the last of her water and strolled back through the gravestones and down the path that passed by the shop. She waved to a couple of Rachel's cousins and was about to turn on to the lane that led to her cottage when she stopped in her tracks. She'd heard him before she saw him.

"All right, darling! Do you know if there's a copper living around here? Goes by the name of Jo. About your height, with green eyes."

Jo cautiously turned the corner and there he was. Detective Sergeant Simon Spencer. Leaning against his gleaming BMW and wearing his dark suit and sunglasses. The top button of his shirt was undone, and he'd loosened the knot of his tie. He thought it made him look edgy. They'd had an on-off relationship for about six months when she'd lived in London. More off than on if she was honest, and now he was here in Hartwell. Talking in his loud London accent, he was addressing Caroline of all people. Jo cringed inwardly. She was fully expecting Caroline to act like he was invisible as she did with most people she considered beneath her. However, instead she gave him a withering look and asked, "What concern are Detective Sergeant Ormond's whereabouts to you?"

Simon removed his glasses and gave her his most charming smile. "She's a mate."

"If that were the case, I rather think you would know her address, wouldn't you?"

Jo took a deep breath and hurried over. "Simon, what are you doing here?"

Caroline and Simon both turned to look at her.

Simon grinned. "Good to see you too, babe."

He wrapped his arms around her and dropped a kiss on

top of her head. Jo breathed in his familiar aftershave and felt a little light-headed. He always wore far too much. She was also acutely aware that Caroline was watching them intently. Jo wriggled out of his embrace.

"Si, this is Caroline. Simon is a friend from London," she explained.

Simon held out his hand, but Caroline ignored it.

"So I see," she replied before turning on her heel and walking away.

"I thought people up north were meant to be friendly," whispered Simon.

"Come on, I live just down here," said Jo. It felt strange having someone from her past here in Hartwell, and she wasn't sure she was ready for him to meet anyone else just yet.

Simon followed her back to the cottage. Jo watched him duck his head as he stepped through the low doorway and looked around, taking in the beamed ceilings, the open fireplace and the cosy kitchen overlooking the rear cottage garden.

"It's a bit different from your old place," he commented.

Jo couldn't disagree. She'd previously lived in Hammersmith, in a tiny, modern flat above an off-licence and a kebab shop. Across the road was a bar and a twenty-four-hour gym. There had been constant noise and thanks to the glaring street lights it was never got properly dark inside either.

"You look great by the way," he said, flashing her his sexiest smile. Jo was well aware she didn't look great and was in fact hot and sweaty after her run.

"I'm going to have a shower," she said. "There's beer in the fridge. Help yourself."

WHEN SHE WENT back downstairs, she found Simon had made himself at home. He was lolling on an old wooden chair in the garden, his jacket off, his feet up on the opposite chair, sipping a beer. She took a second to observe him. There was no denying it—he was a handsome sod. With that blond hair that always fell forward into his pale blue eyes and his charming boyish smile, half the women at Scotland Yard had a crush on him. Unfortunately, he knew it. She popped the top off a bottle of beer and went out to join him.

"So, are you going to tell me what you're doing here?"

He squinted up at her, shielding his eyes from the sun. "Would you believe me if I told you I'd missed you?"

She moved the chair, so his feet hit the ground and sat down herself. "No," she replied bluntly. She was under no illusion that theirs had been one of the world's great romances.

"Okay, I'll tell you all about it. But can we get something to eat first? I'm starving. Is your local any good or shall we call for a takeaway? Do you even have decent takeaways up here?"

"Yes, we have takeaways," she replied tersely, without adding that none of them actually delivered and, for some reason, the thought of taking Simon up to the White Hart filled her with horror. Talk about two worlds colliding. "It'll probably be easier if I make us something."

"Since when did you cook?" he scoffed.

"I'm as capable of turning on an oven as anyone else," she snapped back, getting to her feet and heading back to the kitchen.

"Can I have another beer?" he called after her. She stuck a couple of Meera's ready meals into the oven and silently thanked her neighbour for the hundredth time. She returned with a beer to where Simon was still sunning himself. For a while they chatted about what was happening down in London. They gossiped about colleagues they both knew, who was having an affair with whom, who had been looked over for promotion and whose drinking was getting out of control.

When the food was ready, they moved inside. Jo managed to find two clean plates and forks, then carried the curry and rice through into the sitting room, while Simon opened another couple of beers.

"Did you hear about us arresting Gorton and Kelly?" he asked.

Jo nodded as she recalled the *Evening Standard* report she'd read online.

"Yes, you must have been chuffed. Losing them will be quite a blow to Sutcliffe's organisation," Jo replied, her thoughts automatically drifting to the botched arrest of one of the city's biggest drugs dealers, which had led her to being sent to Yorkshire.

"There's a chance we could get them on more than armed robbery."

"What do you mean?"

Simon gave her a sidelong glance. "The guns they used

were a pair of posh shotguns—Purdeys. We've managed to trace them and they belonged to the late Lord Rupert Hanley. I was thinking, maybe Gorton and Kelly killed His Lordship."

Jo stared at him for a second. Her mind began to race. Her first job when she'd arrived in North Yorkshire was to check all the gun licences in Hartwell. It was when she'd visited Hartwell Hall that she'd discovered that Rupert's guns were missing. At the time, she'd wondered if they could be linked to his disappearance. This new evidence Simon had might lead to the coroner reopening the inquest into his death. What would that mean for Lucy and Rachel?

"That's why you're up here?" she asked.

"Not the only reason," he replied, without looking up from his plate. "I missed having you around. The place isn't the same without your happy, smiling face."

"Very funny!"

"Look, seriously. I thought you'd want to help. You live in the same village as Hanley, you were here when they found the body, and I guessed you'd be bored out of your mind."

"What do you want to know?"

Simon leaned forward. "A while ago, you told me Rupert Hanley had a drug problem."

"That's right. He spent most of his time down in London. Drugs had taken over his life."

"It seems he owed a lot of money to a lot of people, including Sutcliffe. What else can you tell me about him? His body was found in a cave, right?"

"Yep. It was just his skeleton and there were no signs of a

gunshot wound. There isn't much more to say. He disappeared after a meeting in the village hall and wasn't found until the final lockdown restrictions were lifted."

"You've got to have found out more than that."

He was looking at her intently now, but Jo didn't meet his gaze. She wasn't about to start spilling Rachel and Lucy's secrets.

"Not really—besides the coroner recorded an open verdict. He couldn't even be sure what killed him. The case is closed as far as my bosses are concerned."

"That could always change. I'm working on a theory that Gorton and Kelly came up here to get Rupert to pay up. He offered them the guns, but it wasn't enough, or they argued and killed him." He paused. "While I'm up here, I thought I might have a word with Rupert's widow, the lovely Lady Hanley."

"The last thing Lucy needs is to have you turn up on her doorstep," snapped Jo.

Simon raised an eyebrow. "Lucy? It sounds like she's a mate of yours. I never had you down for getting friendly with the aristocracy," he teased.

"She isn't that posh," replied Jo defensively. "But she's had a tough few months."

"Maybe, but it hasn't affected her looks. She's a stunner judging by the pictures I've seen of her."

"You shouldn't judge a book by its cover."

Simon put his plate down and placed an arm around her shoulder. She could feel his fingers playing with her hair.

"I was only joking, Jo," he said softly. "I won't talk to her if you don't want me to."

Jo shrugged him off. He was sitting dangerously close to her now, but she didn't want to be distracted. What they were discussing could affect her future as well as her friends.

"If your theory is right and the case was reopened, it would be a joint investigation between us—between the Met and North Yorkshire?" she pressed. She couldn't believe Palmer, her old boss, would have agreed to such a thing.

Simon dropped his gaze and shifted a little in his seat. "Well, no not exactly. Not in an official way, but we don't have to get into the details right now. Let's talk about it in the morning. I can think of something much better to do." He leaned forward and brushed his lips against her neck. Jo felt a shiver of excitement and lust run through her. "You've always been an amazing detective, Jo," he murmured. "I really wanted to hear your take on all of this, but we can figure out the details in the morning." He stroked her face gently with his finger. They were less than an inch apart.

Jo looked deep into his eyes and didn't like what she saw. She stood up abruptly.

"You haven't even told Palmer about coming to see me, have you?" she asked coldly.

Simon leaned back and sighed but didn't reply.

Jo shook her head. "You want my help, but you'll take all the credit and I'll still be stuck up here."

"Not necessarily, babe," he replied, his tone cajoling.

"Don't babe me," she snapped. "You've always been an arrogant sod."

She stomped out of the room, anger boiling inside her, as she headed up the stairs. Simon came hurrying after her.

"Come on, Jo. Don't be like that," he pleaded, reaching

for her hand, but she shook it off.

"Don't even think about." She pointed back to the sitting room. "You can crash on the sofa and think yourself lucky I don't throw you out."

SHE STILL WASN'T in the mood to speak to him when she woke up at dawn the next morning. Instead, she went downstairs, let the kitchen tap run for a few seconds before filling a cup and then going through to the sitting room. Simon was snoring loudly on the sofa.

"Rise and shine," she called out brightly, flicking the icy water into his face.

He woke up with a start. "Jesus, Jo! What time is it?"

"About six."

"That's the middle of the night. What are you playing at?" He flopped back down.

"You need an early start. It's a long drive back to London," she replied before chucking the rest of the water at him.

"Bloody hell! All right, all right, I'll go; but can I at least have a coffee first?" he asked sitting up and wiping the water from his face.

Jo made him a black coffee while he used the bathroom, then stood silently watching him drink it with her arms folded.

"You do know you've overreacted as usual, don't you?" he said putting down his empty cup. "You are your own worst enemy."

Jo didn't reply, but instead went to open the front door. Simon sighed as he stepped outside. He looked over his shoulder and gave her an evil grin.

"Bye, darlin'. Thanks for last night. You were as amazing as always. Let's do it again some time," he called out as loudly as he could before blowing her a kiss, climbing into his car and revving away.

"Very funny," she muttered. She resisted the temptation to give him the finger and instead stood on the doorstep and made sure he wasn't heading towards Hartwell Hall and Lucy. She turned around and was about to step back inside when she saw someone standing on the other side of the lane. Jack watching her with an expression that could only be described as heartbroken. He'd obviously heard what Simon said.

"Jack!" she called out. "It's not what you think."

His big brown eyes stared at her blankly for a second, then he turned and quickly limped away.

"Wait," she shouted again and started to go after him, only to realise her feet were bare and she was only wearing an oversized T-shirt. Swearing under her breath, she tiptoed over the stones back into her cottage and ran upstairs. Bloody selfish Simon! She replayed his departure in her head and knew exactly what it must have looked like. She also knew how Jack felt about her—he'd told her plenty of times. He deserved an explanation. She pulled on her jeans and a pair of trainers.

By the time she reached the pub, she was out of breath. She knocked loudly on the door and waited. She had no idea what she was going to say to Jack. But it wasn't him who opened the door. It was Rachel, her face full of fury.

"How could you?" she demanded before Jo even had chance to open her mouth. "You know how he feels about you. If you were going to get back with an old boyfriend, you could have at least warned him."

"I can explain," protested Jo. "You see Simon wanted to talk to me about a case in London."

Rachel threw her hands up in the air. "Oh London, London, London. That's all you care about. If your job is so bloody important to you, why don't you do us all a favour and go back down there."

Rachel had turned red in the face and Jo began to back away from her as she continued to scream and shout. Normally, she would stick up for herself, but she knew that what Rachel was yelling was true and she couldn't get the image of Jack's heartbroken face out of her head. Shirley suddenly appeared at the doorway of the pub wearing her dressing gown.

"That's enough, Rachel. Half the village can hear you," she hissed.

"Can I talk to Jack?" Jo pleaded.

"He's gone for a walk with Baxter," said Shirley.

Jo turned to go after him. There were only so many directions he could have taken, but Shirley called her back.

"I think it might be better to leave him on his own right now, love."

Jo looked from Shirley's apologetic smile to Rachel's still-furious face. She nodded silently and trudged back to the cottage. The curtains were open at Meera's.

"Can I come in?" she asked in a quiet voice when Meera

opened the door.

"Yes, of course. Are you okay? You don't look very well." Meera ushered her in past half-filled packing boxes. "Come and sit down in the kitchen and I'll make us a cup of tea."

"I've messed up, Meera. An old boyfriend came to see me yesterday and now Jack is upset."

Meera nodded. "I know. I heard your guest leave."

"Did you see Jack too?"

"Yes, I looked out of the window to see what was going on and saw him there. He looked devastated."

"Nothing happened with Simon. He was only trying to embarrass me, but I've got to explain that to Jack and I don't think he wants to talk to me right now."

Meera was quiet for a moment. "Perhaps you should think carefully about what you want to say, before you speak to him."

"What do you mean?"

"Well, explaining to him that nothing happened with you and Simon." She handed Jo a cup of tea. "It might be kinder to let him think something did. If he doesn't stand a chance with you, it could be easier for him to move on if he believes there's someone else."

"You think I've been leading him on?" asked Jo.

Meera shook her head. "No, not exactly, but it's no secret how he feels about you, but you don't feel the same. He looked so upset when he saw Simon leaving. Why give him hope, only to break his heart again, when you do return to London or even meet someone else? Perhaps this might be a blessing in disguise."

JO SPENT THE rest of the day sitting in the cottage with the curtains closed. Occasionally, she sneaked out to the church to sit by her favourite gravestone and have a smoke. Although her eyes barely left the White Hart, there was no sign of Jack. She kept mulling over what Meera had said. Part of her knew it made sense, but it was no good—she couldn't go to bed without speaking to him. He'd only ever treated her with kindness. Whatever else she did, he deserved an apology.

As it began to grow dark outside, she made a decision. She'd wait until he'd finished work and go and speak to him.

SHE'D NEVER KNOWN time to pass so slowly, but now it was almost eleven. He'd be calling last orders soon. She'd be able to speak to him when everyone else had left. Grabbing her coat, she headed out the door and up the lane to the White Hart. As she approached, she noticed Rob and Dan— Rachel's cousin—were sitting at one of the tables outside. As much as she liked them, she wasn't in the mood for a chat. She decided to go through the side gate and enter the pub through the beer garden.

She had her hand on the gate when Dan stood up and said goodbye to Rob. He walked to his Land Rover and Rob was about to drain his own pint, when Sadie appeared at the front door. She was carrying a glass of wine and a pint of beer and made her way over to Rob's table.

"I really should be going," Jo heard him say, only for Sadie to pout and flick her hair back.

"Surely you have time for one tiny drinky with me?" She slipped into the seat next to him. "I wanted to talk to you about Lucy."

"Why? Is something wrong?" he asked.

Jo listened with a growing feeling of unease. Then she remembered what Meera and Rachel had both said. Lucy wouldn't thank her for interfering when it came to Sadie. Maybe it was better if she didn't know what was going on. Reluctantly, she moved slowly back to the gate and slipped through into the garden. Through the side window she could see Shirley trying to encourage the three farmers at the bar to finish their drinks. Jo moved on towards the back door and stopped.

Through the rear window she could she Jack in the games room, but he wasn't alone. Becky was there too. Her long blonde hair hanging loose with her hand raised to her mouth, she was giggling at something Jack must have said. What was she doing here? Then Jo remembered she worked there now, but she couldn't remember Chloe—the other waitress—staying behind to play snooker. Jack handed Becky a cue and was clearly trying to line up a shot for her.

Jo watched as Becky missed and started giggling again. Jack gave her a quick hug. Becky looked happier than she had in a long time and Jack certainly didn't seem heartbroken any longer. Jo winced. Seeing them together like this was physically painful. As an extra blow, Baxter came scampering into the games room, his tail wagging happily. What had she expected to find? Jack alone and crying into his beer? He was kind and funny. Everybody loved him. Why the hell would he be on his own?

She watched as Jack went over to the old stereo in the corner. A few seconds later she could hear the faint hum of music, Oasis it sounded like. Jack loved nineties music. How many times had she spent an evening with him in there laughing, dancing and half-heartedly playing snooker? Now Becky was in her place, and it hurt more than she could ever have imagined. Meera was right. Seeing her with Simon had made Jack realise there was no future with her, and he'd moved on. Tears blinded her eyes. She'd been such a fool.

Backing quietly away from the window, she turned and hurried quietly way. She was so upset she didn't even notice that Rob and Sadie were nowhere to be seen.

CHAPTER FOURTEEN

S O FAR, THE summer had been a huge success. Eight weddings, two magazine photo shoots and this morning she'd signed the contract for another period drama to start shooting later in the year. To her great surprise, Lucy was actually enjoying her new role, even if it did mean stepping over cables that trailed across the floor, constantly dodging around camera equipment and even reassuring the occasional nervous bride.

She had been busy all morning, checking everything was in order for the day's filming. As she reached the drawing room, she could hear Sadie speaking on the phone to someone.

"That sounds terribly interesting, but I'm afraid we aren't able to offer the hall for your event. We're fully booked."

"What was that all about?" asked Lucy, as her mother put down the receiver. Sadie looked around in surprise.

"Oh, nothing to worry about, darling. It was just some women's refuge wanting to use the hall free of charge for a fundraising event."

"The Rosemary Centre?" queried Lucy.

"Yes, that's the one, darling. Honestly, the cheek of some

people. Don't worry, I told them nicely that you're running a business here. They won't call again. Now, how about a nice G&T? Then I thought I'd have a lovely long soak in the bath."

"No, not for me thanks, Mum. I need to drive later, but you go ahead."

As soon as she'd gone, Lucy picked up the phone and called back the last number. It was answered by a woman named Alison, who after Lucy had introduced herself, explained that she was head of fundraising at the Rosemary Centre.

The Rosemary Centre was located in Thirsk and was one of the few women's refuges for victims of domestic abuse in rural North Yorkshire. It had been set up over thirty years ago by the friends and family of Rosemary, a young woman who had been beaten to death by her husband, a serving police officer. Lucy thought it was one of the area's most deserving charities and if she could help in any way she would.

"I understand that you wanted to book Hartwell Hall?" said Lucy.

"Yes, we wanted to hold a drinks reception there, but I hear you already have booking. It's the last Friday in August," explained Alison.

Lucy quickly began flicking through the pocket diary that was constantly wedged in the back pocket of her jeans.

"Unfortunately, yes. The hall is being used for a photo shoot that day, but—" she glanced across to the day before "—there will be a marquee in the grounds. It's being used on the day before and the day after, but it's free on that day. It seats a hundred. Would that be any good?"

"That sounds wonderful. Thank you very much."

"No problem and if there's anything else I can do to help, do please let me know."

"Actually," said Alison, hesitating slightly, "would you and a guest be able to attend the event? You see we are struggling to get publicity and if I could tell the local press..." She trailed off, but Lucy knew what she was getting at. Her title wasn't much good for anything except attracting attention, particularly in the press.

"I'd be delighted to attend," replied Lucy, although she had no idea who she'd take as her guest.

As soon as she put the phone down, she heard Freddie calling her name. They had arranged to go for a long walk with the dogs. There was an important scene being filmed in the ballroom today and the director had not very subtly suggested things might go more smoothly if Tilly, Root and Pickle weren't in the vicinity.

"Isn't Granny Sadie coming with us?" asked Freddie as they and the dogs headed out of the kitchen.

"No, darling, I don't think walks are really her thing." Lucy sighed. She'd given up asking Sadie to join them. There was no way she'd want to tramp through the countryside when she could be loitering around the handsome actors on the film set.

"She likes walking to the White Hart," said Freddie, "maybe it's only daytime walks she doesn't like. She does spend a lot of the day asleep. Like a vampire."

"Freddie!" exclaimed Lucy. "Granny Sadie is not a vam-pire!"

"I know that. I'm just saying they don't like daylight either. Or garlic."

Lucy decided to change the subject as they made their way towards the lake. "How's your batting coming along?" she asked. Freddie and Krish had joined the weekly cricket sessions that Jack and the colonel ran every year for the children in the village. Lucy had signed him up at the start of the summer as a distraction from everything else that was going on.

"Good, but my bowling action needs some work. Rob said he'd help. Is he coming over today?"

"Yes, I think so. He's bringing someone to look at the roof later this afternoon," replied Lucy.

"Great! Does that mean we can get a takeaway?"

"Yes, I expect so," Lucy said with a laugh.

Over the last few weeks Rob had spent rather a lot of time with them. He'd been a huge help with finding all the false invoices and claims Max had made and usually ended up staying for supper with her and Freddie. Lucy was the first to admit she wasn't a great cook and after stoically working his way through a plate of burnt sausages and a still frozen in the middle cottage pie, Rob had given up.

"Sorry, Lucy," he'd said on his third visit, "Freddie and I have had a vote and we've decided to get a takeaway tonight."

"Really?" Lucy had replied innocently. "I was thinking of making moussaka tonight."

Rob and Freddie had exchanged a look of horror before bursting out laughing.

"Come on, Freddie, let's go to Thirsk before she carries

out her threat," Rob had said and the two of them had headed out the door.

Since that night, they'd fallen into a routine of getting a takeaway once a week, then curling up with the dogs in the library to watch a film. Lucy found Rob took being strong and silent to another level. He could quite easily not say a word for over an hour. When she realised that this didn't mean he was upset or in a bad mood, she had started to enjoy the companionable silence.

The other night they had been watching *Jurassic Park* with Freddie for what seemed like the hundredth time. Even Sadie had decided to join them, curling up on the other sofa with a large glass of red wine. As the T-Rex rampaged the across the screen, Rob's outstretched arm had rested along Lucy's shoulders and it had felt like the most natural thing in the world.

Sometimes, now Lucy no longer needed assistance with the accounts, Rob would help Freddie with his cricket or simply listen to her plans for the estate. He rarely expressed an opinion unless she asked him. The exception was when she'd told him about Max disappearing to Spain. He'd obviously been furious on her behalf.

"I guess I should have listened to you and confronted him earlier," Lucy had admitted regretfully.

Rob had clenched his jaw and shaken his head. "It's not your fault. He took us all in. I had him down as incompetent not corrupt."

Although nothing had happened between them, she often found herself daydreaming what it would be like if they were more than friends. When he was busy with Freddie, she would sneak the occasional appreciative glance in his direction. He really was ridiculously handsome.

ROB BROUGHT THE builder over later that afternoon and the two of them spent an hour on the roof. Lucy went up too and watched with a sinking heart as the builder poked and prodded and kept shaking his head. However, when he finally climbed down and gave her a quote it was almost half the figure Max had provided her with.

"Thank you so much for recommending him," she said turning to smile at Rob, who was standing next to her as she waved the builder goodbye. "I can't believe I'll finally be able to get the roof fixed. Shall we order a takeaway to celebrate? Your choice, Indian or Chinese?"

Rob, however, didn't return her smile. "I can't tonight. I've got something on."

Lucy was surprised how disappointed she felt. "Oh well, never mind. Maybe another time," she said, but Rob didn't reply and instead started walking towards his car.

"Actually, I have another favour to ask before you go." Rob stopped and turned to look at her. He was frowning, but she couldn't work out why. "The Rosemary Centre are hosting an event here and they want me to go along and to bring a guest. It's at the end of August, black tie. I thought you might like to come along, if you are free. It's for a good cause."

"You want me to go with you?"

His tone was so cold it almost made her shiver. She'd

been a little apprehensive about asking him, but she never dreamed his response would be this negative. She started chewing her lip nervously.

"Yes. I know it might be a bit of a bore, but I promised I'd go..." She trailed off. Rob was still frowning. She saw his eyes travel over her shoulder to where Sadie was sitting in the window humming along to the radio as she flicked through a magazine.

Rob turned back to Lucy and sighed. "Okay. If you're sure that's what you want. See you later."

"See you later," echoed Lucy. She stood and watched him walk back to his car. She couldn't work out why he was behaving so strangely. Had she done something wrong? She gave her head a shake. This is exactly why she shouldn't even think about getting into another relationship. She was already starting to blame herself for the way Rob was acting.

Taking a deep breath, she went inside to find Freddie. There was no reason for them not to still order a takeaway and tonight he could choose.

"Is Rob not staying for supper?" Sadie called out.

"No," replied Lucy, "not tonight."

"Oh well, just the three of us. How lovely!"

CHAPTER FIFTEEN

M EERA CLOSED THE door behind her last patient. The day was almost over. Once she had written up her notes she could go and collect Krish from the holiday club. After Jo had confirmed that Darren would be remaining in custody, she had been happy for her son to return there. Ben was due home that evening and when she popped home to collect the post during her morning break, she had found the solicitors had sent the contract for the Grange. After all that panic and worry of the last couple of weeks, it felt like her life was finally back on track. The sound of urgent knocking at her door made her look up in surprise.

"Come in," she called out and then jumped up when Ben came through the door.

"You're home early!" she exclaimed in delight, throwing her arms around him. "Oh I've missed you."

She lifted her face to kiss him, but he stepped back.

"I missed you too, Meera. But what's going on? I got home early and had some good news. I thought I'd collect Krish as a surprise, but the teacher on duty said I couldn't because I didn't have permission."

Meera's hand flew to her mouth. "Oh, I'm sorry. That's my fault. Something happened while you were away, and I made the school promise not to let anyone collect Krish except me. You'd better sit down and I'll explain."

Ben took the seat opposite her desk and stared at her incredulously as she began to recount what had happened.

"Why on earth didn't you tell me? I'd have come home straight away."

"That's why I didn't say anything. I did think about it, but whenever you called the line kept breaking up and it wasn't the sort of thing I wanted to put in an email." She paused. "And I didn't want you to think me wanting to protect Krish had anything to do with my decision to move in with you."

"I would never have thought that. As far as I'm concerned, we're a team. I want to protect him every bit as much as you do." He shook his head. "You must have been so worried. I hate to think of you coping with it all on your own."

"I know I should have told you, but I wasn't totally alone. Jo and Nish were great."

"I thought you didn't get on with your brother."

"I think I may have underestimated him," she admitted.

"Are you sure this Darren person is no longer a threat to you or Krish?"

"Positive. Jo said he won't get bail because of his previous convictions and the drugs they found are class A, so he'll be facing a long sentence."

"Good," said Ben then he reached over and took hold of her hands. "Meera, I want you to promise me if anything like this happens again, you'll let me know. Whatever the circumstances, I want to be the person you call when there's an emergency. I want to take care of you and Krish. We'll be living together soon, and I really want us to be a proper family."

Seeing the hurt in his eyes, Meera was stung with guilt. Jo was right—she should have told him.

She squeezed his hands. "That's what I want too," she assured him. "That's why I've asked Dev for a divorce and he's actually agreed."

Ben's face lit up. "Really? That's wonderful news."

"Yes. As we've already been separated for two years, it should only take four months, six at the most."

Ben adjusted his glasses and squinted at the calendar on the wall. "So that would mean either Christmas or Valentine's Day. I suppose either would work."

"What are you talking about?"

"Our wedding. Christmas would make the most sense because we are both already off work and Krish isn't at school, but if it takes longer, we could go for Valentine's Day."

Meera stared at him open-mouthed. "Our wedding?" she repeated.

"Yes. Four months would take us to Christmas and six months would be Valentine's Day. Both seem equally romantic to me, but the main thing is it would be a winter wedding. Or would you rather wait until the summer?"

"But we haven't discussed it," stammered Meera.

"Do we need to? I assumed it was understood we'd get married as soon as your divorce came through. Don't you want to? Do you need more time? I understand if you don't want to rush into another marriage."

He looked crestfallen and Meera felt another pang of guilt. Although she usually loved Ben's practical no-nonsense approach to life, how could she explain that she did want to marry him, but she had hoped for a little more romance when it came to discussing their wedding? Sitting in her office looking at a calendar from a surgical glove company wasn't quite what she had dreamed of.

"It isn't that I don't want to," she said gently. "Look, perhaps this isn't the best time to talk about it. Didn't you say you had some good news too?"

Ben slapped his forehead. "Yes, I almost forgot. I spoke to the estate agents earlier. I've arranged for us to rent the Grange for the next few weeks while the paperwork for the sale is completed. It means we can move in almost straight away."

Meera leaned forward and kissed him again. "That is good news. Let's go and collect Krish together and tell him."

"I'M SORRY I couldn't stay longer. Krish and I have been very happy here. I feel terribly guilty leaving you," said Meera as she handed the spare keys back to Lucy. Today was the day they were moving into the Grange, only as tenants at first, but if everything went according to plan, it would be theirs in a few weeks.

Lucy grinned at her. "You don't look remotely sorry, Meera. In fact, I don't think I've seen you happier."

Meera began to protest.

"I'm joking, Meera," Lucy reassured her, "and you have

nothing to apologise for. You gave me the required notice and I've started advertising for a new tenant."

"I hope you find someone soon. Krish and I have been very happy here. Are you dealing with all the estate properties yourself now, well now Max has gone?" asked Meera.

However, before Lucy could reply, they heard and familiar loud voice call out, "Lucinda! There you are!"

"Oh no, oh no," groaned Lucy, pointlessly pulling her baseball cap further down over her face. "Here comes Caroline. I've been trying to avoid her. Last night I told the colonel I couldn't hold the fete at the Hall this year. She's bound to have heard by now."

Meera turned to look down the lane. Sure enough Caroline was striding towards them with a face like thunder.

"Good morning, Lady Hanley," said Meera with a polite smile as Lucy continued to cower next to her.

"Good morning, Dr Kumar," replied Caroline briskly, before turning her attention to her daughter-in-law.

"There you are, Lucinda," she repeated. "What's this I hear about not being able to hold the village fete at Hartwell Hall?"

"I'm really sorry, Caroline, but I took a booking for a wedding that weekend. I forgot all about the fete," stammered Lucy.

Caroline threw up her hands in despair. "How could you be this hopeless? The Hall always holds the fete. What are we meant to do now?"

Lucy began apologising again.

Meera watched with sympathy, then suddenly an idea came to her. "Actually, Lady Hanley," she interrupted, "Lucy just made a rather wonderful suggestion that might solve your problem."

"Really?" replied Caroline, looking extremely sceptical at Lucy being capable of such a thing.

"Did I?" asked Lucy under her breath, looking very puzzled.

"Yes," replied Meera smoothly. "She thought it would be a good idea to hold the fete at the Grange. As I'm sure you know, Ben and I are about to move in. It's only a little farther out of the village, but the lawn is lovely and flat."

Caroline's cold blue eyes travelled slowly between the innocent smiling faces of the two younger women for several seconds, before she inclined her head slightly.

"Well, it's not ideal, but I suppose it might work, for one year only, and thanks to Lucinda's appalling ability to plan, we have very little choice. Thank you, Dr Kumar. I shall inform the rest of the committee that disaster has been averted. In the meantime, Lucinda, please could you speak with your mother? Whilst I appreciate she may want to make up for lost time now she has finally arrived in Hartwell and no doubt wants to get to know some of your friends and acquaintances, she ought to remember the colonel is a respected member of the community, a widower and is not a well man. It really isn't appropriate for her to be drinking and galivanting with him until the early hours of the morning. She may also want to revise the way she dresses and find something more suitable to wear in a village in England rather than St Tropez or wherever it is she normally resides. After all, she does represent the Hanley family even if it is only by association."

Without waiting for a response, Caroline turned and walked briskly away.

"I'll have a word with her," Lucy called out then exhaled loudly, as she disappeared from sight. "Wow! Thank you, Meera. You are an absolute lifesaver! What about Ben, though? Are you sure he won't mind?"

"No of course he won't," Meera replied confidently. "He was only saying the other day how much he likes Hartwell and how good it will feel to be part of the village."

LATER THAT AFTERNOON, Meera and Ben were busy packing in preparation for the move. Ben had already moved all his things out of his flat and into the Grange and they had been living in a kind of limbo between there and the cottage. Ben was sitting on the floor while Meera was carefully wrapping and placing her favourite ornaments in a large cardboard box.

"Ben," she began a little cautiously, "you know how we talked about having a housewarming party for all our friends in the village when we move into the Grange?"

"Yes," replied Ben without looking up from the newspaper he was trying to read before Meera used it for wrapping. "I said we should do it before we start redecorating so it doesn't matter if they make a mess. Not that it would bother me, but you wouldn't relax if you thought someone was about to spill red wine on a new carpet."

"That is true," admitted Meera. "Well I thought I'd kill two birds with one stone. Invite everyone over and get Lucy out of Caroline's bad books."

He looked up with a puzzled expression.

"I've offered to host the village fete at the Grange," she explained, hoping her instincts were right and he wouldn't mind. She was still feeling guilty about not telling him about Dev. To her relief, he simply shrugged and nodded.

"Fine with me. I went to the fete a couple of years ago. It was good fun. Don't you think though, if you are making such a public statement that you should let your parents know about us moving in together? You know, before they hear it from someone else."

Meera carefully placed the latest ornament in the box and sighed. "I know, I know, I just need to pick the right time."

"At least we don't have to worry about my parents. One is miles away and one is dead."

"Ben!"

"What?"

"It sounds a bit heartless when you put it that bluntly."

"I'm not being heartless, it's true. Dad is dead and Mum is out in Australia visiting my sister."

"Does she know we are moving in together? Should I introduce myself? Do a video call or something with her?"

"Yes, she knows we're going to be living together and no you shouldn't Skype her or whatever. She hates technology. She wouldn't thank you for making her sit in front of a computer screen."

"What if she doesn't like me when she meets me?"

"Why would she not like you? You are kind, intelligent, polite—all the things that matter to her. Besides even if she did take a dislike to you, it wouldn't stop me wanting to live with you."

Meera leaned across and kissed him on the cheek.

"Thank you. You make it sound very simple."

"That's because it is. Trust me, the sooner you speak to your parents the better."

"What do you need to speak to Granny and Grandpa about?" asked Krish as he carefully carried a box of his books down the stairs. Ben stood up to help him.

"Lots of things," replied Meera, then seeing Ben raise his eyebrows meaningfully over the box: "Why don't you come and sit next to me for a minute, and I'll tell you."

"I'll go and put this in the car," said Ben as he diplomatically left the room. Krish flopped down on the sofa next to his mother. Meera cleared her throat. This was another conversation she had been putting off, but Ben was right—she couldn't avoid it forever.

"There are a few things I need to tell Granny and Grandpa. Firstly, that Ben will be living with us and that we are moving to the Grange."

"I think they'll be pleased," said Krish. "The Grange is great and it's much bigger than here so they can come and stay with us."

"That's true," agreed Meera. "But there is something else I need to tell them and you. Your dad and I have decided to get divorced. How do you feel about that?" she asked as her mouth turned dry.

Her son creased his forehead in concentration for a few moments. He was clearly giving the matter some serious thought. "Will I have to change my name?" he asked finally.

Meera shook her head and smiled. "No of course not. Nothing will change for you. Your father will always be your father and you can see him or speak to him whenever you want, but I won't be married to him anymore."

"Will you and Ben get married?"

"I'm not sure. Perhaps we might one day. Would you mind?"

"No. That would be cool. Except…" he paused and Meera held her breath "…you wouldn't make me be a pageboy would you? Freddie showed me a picture of him when he was a pageboy for one of Lucy's friends when he was about four. They made him wear blue satin. It was really cringe."

Meera bit her lip to stop herself laughing. "I promise I will never make you wear blue satin, Krish."

"Okay then," said Krish standing up and making his way to the door. "I'm going to see if Ben needs any help."

Meera watched him go and gave a sigh of relief. She only hoped the conversation she had with her parents would go so well.

CHAPTER SIXTEEN

RACHEL TOOK A deep breath and leaned back in the saddle. This is exactly what she needed. The space and freedom of the moors stretching out as far as her eye could see. It felt good to be out in the open, away from everyone.

She had collected Bailey from Dan's, and the two of them had hacked to the top of the moor that rose up behind her cousin's farm. It was late afternoon, later than she would normally set off. The air was heavy and humid. A storm had been forecast for that evening. Dark clouds were gathering, but Rachel didn't care. They suited her mood.

It was Saturday when everything had started to go wrong. She'd woken early and left Sarah sleeping soundly while she went to make some tea. Sarah had arrived late the night before with a car full of her things. Funding for her research project based on the Druid burial site was due to be granted any day and they had agreed that it made sense for her to stay with Rachel during the week at least.

The two of them had barely been apart since Sarah returned to the village. For Rachel, it had felt almost perfect. There had only been a couple of awkward moments. Rachel often had nightmares about the night Rupert disappeared. They were always the same. She would relive seeing a panic-stricken Lucy returning to Hartwell Hall and then see herself driving to the building site expecting to find a dead body, but only recovering the bloodstained spade she'd flung down the well.

What Rachel hadn't realised was that she also talked in her sleep. Twice over the last few weeks, Sarah had woken her up asking if she was okay and telling her she'd been calling out Rupert and Lucy's names. Rachel had tried to make light of it. Telling Sarah the business with Max and the police must have triggered memories of when they were in Hartwell looking for Rupert. Sarah had held her close, stroking her hair and comforting her, but Rachel wasn't entirely sure she believed her story.

The two of them had planned to spend that Saturday unpacking and Rachel wanted to surprise her with breakfast in bed. However, one sniff of the milk in the fridge told her it had gone off. At the same time she heard her uncle Frank, the local milkman, delivering to the White Hart.

She'd dashed outside, but before she could catch up with her uncle, she'd seen Jack heading back to the pub. He looked close to tears. She was shocked. The last time she'd seen him cry was when he was about four years old and Rupert had stolen his favourite football. She'd chased after him and ignored his attempts to tell her he was fine. Finally, she cornered him in the pub kitchen and got the story of how he'd set off that morning, hoping to go for his usual jog with Jo, only to find her waving goodbye to another man, who made it quite clear he'd spent the night with her.

"How could she be so cruel?" howled Rachel, furious on behalf of her oldest, kindest and most lovable friend, but

Jack simply shook his head.

"It's not Jo's fault, Rach. She's always said she didn't want to get involved with me, that she wanted to get back to her old life in London. I've been a total idiot. I can't help it. I'm mad about her. I know she didn't feel the same way about me, but seeing her with someone else, I don't know, it was like she'd slapped me in the face." He attempted a smile. "And to be quite honest, I'd prefer it if she had."

"What are you going to do?" she asked.

Jack sighed. "Long term, no idea. Short term, go for a very long walk."

"Shall I come with you?"

"No offence, Rach, but I feel like being on my own right now, except for Baxter of course." He whistled and the young Labrador came hurtling into the kitchen. "Come on, lad. Let's go!"

Rachel had watched him and Baxter lollop down the garden and towards the moors, wishing she could think of a way to make him feel better. Then Jo had the cheek to turn up, pretending that she cared. Rachel had told her exactly what she thought of her and for once her feisty friend hadn't been able to defend herself.

When she had returned to the cottage, Sarah was awake, but instead of eating breakfast or unpacking, Rachel found her in the sitting room surrounded by photos of Lucy. Rachel groaned inwardly. They had been stashed in a drawer and she'd completely forgotten about them. She'd collected them when she'd harboured her secret infatuation.

"I thought the two of you were just friends," Sarah had said quietly.

"We are," protested Rachel. Sarah turned to look and her and shook her head. Her face was pale and her eyes brimming with hurt.

"I don't secretly hoard photos of my friends. I don't call out their names in the night either."

"Nothing has ever happened between us."

"But you wanted it to. I knew it. The first time we met, when we'd discovered the skeleton, you were desperate to go and see how she was. When I asked you to come with me to Peru, your excuse was that you had to be here for Lucy."

Sarah almost spat out her name. Rachel opened her mouth to explain, but how could she? It would mean telling Sarah everything that had happened that night with Rupert. Besides it was true that for a long time she had been in love with Lucy or thought that she had been. She wanted to say that since being with Sarah, she'd realised that what she felt for Lucy had been a silly obsession, but in the end, all she'd managed to say was: "I'm sorry."

Sarah hadn't said another word. She'd just walked out and driven away. Rachel had kept trying her mobile all weekend, but she wouldn't pick up. She'd driven over to York, but there was no sign of life at her flat. When she returned to Hartwell, she decided she had a choice to either curl up under her duvet constantly checking her phone or go for a ride.

She and Bailey had now reached Moorhead Farm, one of the estate properties that was never used except as shelter for the occasional shooting party. It was one of the places Max had used to try and defraud Lucy. Rachel dismounted and led Bailey into the farmyard, hoping to find a water trough for him to drink from. She was in luck. In the corner of the yard was a large stone tank beneath a rusty old tap.

While he drank noisily, she leant against the old gate and stared out across the moors. How many of her ancestors had looked at the same view? It was only recently that she had begun to appreciate how connected she was to the landscape. Thanks to Sarah, she'd begun reading up on the history of Hartwell. Time and time again the name Foxton kept appearing in documents, sometimes centuries old.

With a growing sense of pride, she realised the village really was in her blood and that sleepy old Hartwell had once been incredibly important to the ancient Celts. She'd even started wearing the Foxton Hartwell noble around her neck like Jo did. How wonderful it would have been if she and Sarah could have shown the rest of the world how special it was. They had spent hours discussing, arguing and laughing about all the possibilities. Sarah was funny and clever and generous with her ideas and knowledge. And know she was gone.

A tear rolled down Rachel's face. She brushed it away with the back of her hand. At the same time, there was a loud rumble of thunder over her head. Heavy raindrops began to fall, mingling in with her tears. A loud whinny from Bailey made her turn around. Her old pony was tossing his head and stamping his feet. He was not a fan of thunderstorms. They would have to shelter.

Grabbing his reins, she led him towards the stables but the roof was leaking so badly they may as well stay outside. Peering around through the now pouring rain, her eyes stopped on the back door of the farmhouse. Was it her imagination, or was it slightly open? Turning back, they splashed through the puddles towards the farmhouse. Yes, it was wedged shut, but not fully closed. The old doorframe must have become too damp and swollen. Whoever was last there must have given up and not bothered to lock it. When she gave it a hefty shove with her shoulder, it opened and she stumbled inside. Bailey obediently trotted after her, shaking the water from his mane.

Rachel blinked and pushed a few loose strands of hair away from her face. It was cold, dark and damp in the old kitchen, but at least it was dry. She must remember to tell Lucy about the door. There was a flash of lightning followed by a loud crash of thunder. She put her hand on Bailey's neck and rested her head against him.

"Shush, now. It's all right. It'll be over soon," she whispered softly, breathing in his lovely horsey smell. Then she lifted her head. There was something else she could smell. Smoke! She sniffed again. Yes, she could definitely smell smoke. Could the lightning have struck the farmhouse? *Please don't let it be on fire!* She already knew she couldn't get a signal up here to call for help.

She glanced around and suddenly noticed a wisp of smoke from the old open grate. She moved closer and peered down. There was a single tiny glowing ember and drops of water splashed on the surrounding tiles. Somebody had rushed to put the fire out. At that moment there was a creaking sound from upstairs. Rachel edged towards the rickety old staircase in the corner of the kitchen and she looked up into the gloomy darkness.

"Hello? Who's there?" she called out in a shaking voice.

There was another flash of lightning and suddenly she saw him standing at the top of the stairs.

"I should have known it would be you, you nosy cow!" he growled.

"Max? What the hell are you doing here?" she gasped. Could it really be him? He was unshaven and his usually slicked-back blond hair was falling across his face.

"Always interfering! You can't stop yourself."

He was coming down the stairs now. Rachel began to back slowly away.

"We thought you were in Spain," she stammered. Her mind was racing. Had he come back for Becky and Minty? There was a dangerous glint in his eyes. What if he tried to harm Mary? How could she warn them?

"Well for once you were wrong," he snarled. There was no trace of his stupid fake accent now and he was dressed in jeans and a grubby black hoodie. He had reached the bottom of the stairs. There were only a few feet between them. His fists were clenched tightly.

"I had it all worked out. Me and Becky could have had the life we deserved, instead of worrying about money all the time. We'd have still looked after your mother. Why couldn't you have buggered off to South America with your bloody girlfriend? Who the hell do you think you are? You stupid…"

His last word was lost in another crash of thunder. Rachel opened her mouth to protest as his fist connected with her jaw. He hit her with such force that blood immediately spurted out of her lips. She stumbled back with the shock and pain. He came for her again. She dodged out of the way and made a grab at his knees. He fell to the floor too with an angry shout. Rachel tried to get to her feet, but she felt too weak and dizzy. Bailey reared up, and the next thing Rachel saw was her horse's hooves crashing down on to Max. Then everything went black.

THERE WAS WARM breath blowing on her face. Rachel slowly opened her eyes and Bailey's brown velvety nose gradually came into focus. She could taste blood in her mouth and her head was throbbing. She was lying in darkness, but in the distance she could hear people calling her name.

CHAPTER SEVENTEEN

JO STARED OUT of the open office window. It was a blisteringly hot day, with barely a breath of wind. Two wood pigeons sat in the tree opposite her, cooing to each other. She wished they would bloody well shut up. She picked up a staple and took aim, then immediately put it back down again and spun her chair around. It wasn't their fault she was in such a bad mood. Her misery was totally self-inflicted. She'd taken Jack for granted and now he'd found someone else.

Her moping was interrupted by a loud voice. "Sarge! Sarge! Jo!"

Jo looked up. Dawson was hurrying towards her. She guessed he had come up from the canteen. He was red in the face, short of breath, and the remnants of a sausage roll were still stuck to his chin.

"What's up?" she asked.

"I think Lord Rupert Hanley might still be alive."

She gave him a withering look. She was far too hot and miserable to listen to his nonsense.

"What are you talking about? His body was identified using DNA."

"Passport control flagged it up. Someone using his passport has passed through Leeds Bradford Airport. What else could it mean?"

Jo stared back at her hapless colleague as she let this information sink in before she replied.

"It means Max is still alive and he's back in the country."

"What? How do you know that?" asked Dawson as he leaned against her desk, trying to catch his breath.

"Who else do we know who had access to the estate office, needed to disappear quickly and is dishonest enough to steal a dead man's passport? He wasn't to know Rupert's name was still on the airport security list after he disappeared. Get CCTV images sent over from the airport to confirm though."

She glanced up at Dawson's sweaty face, which was creased in confusion.

"Never mind. I'll do it."

She phoned the airport security desk and asked them to forward footage from the time Dawson had scribbled down. She waited impatiently, drumming her fingers on the desk while Dawson's breathing returned to normal until an email pinged on to her screen. She watched the footage intently of the arrivals from Malaga. There he was. Looking dishevelled and scruffy, he stuck out in the crowd of smiling holiday-makers with their shorts and sunburnt faces.

"I'd better phone Becky and let her know in case he tries to contact her," she said reluctantly. She hated the thought of having to talk to the woman who had taken her place in Jack's heart. Dawson, who was watching the screen over her shoulder, nodded. Perhaps he could be useful for once.

"Actually, maybe you could phone her, while I contact

Lucy Hanley. There's always a chance he might return to somewhere on the estate instead of the village," she suggested casually.

"Okay, boss. Why do you think he came back?" asked her colleague, flopping into the chair next to her.

"I imagine, thanks to Rachel's efficiency, his bank accounts and credit cards were shut down more quickly than he expected," she explained.

Dawson still looked puzzled as he reached for the phone.

"To put it bluntly he ran out of money. I bet the Costa del Sol isn't as much fun if you are skint," she added.

Jo picked up her phone and dialled Lucy's number. She picked up almost immediately and greeted Jo with the words: "Oh no! What's happened?"

"I'm fine thanks, Lucy. How are you?" replied Jo sarcastically.

"Sorry, Jo, but you don't usually ring me for a girly gossip and when you do call it does tend to be with bad news."

"Okay, fair point. I do have news, but I'm not sure if it's good or bad yet. Max is back in the country. I thought you would want to know in case he turned up somewhere on the estate. You might want to check any empty buildings and beef up the security at the Hall."

"Thanks, I will—and I'll send an email to all our tenants and let them know, but I don't think he'll come back to Hartwell. Too many people would recognise him, and he doesn't know that neither the estate nor Mary are pressing charges. It would be too big a risk. I bet he's gone back to Manchester. It's easier to be anonymous in a big city."

"It is," agreed Jo. "You could be right. I'll let you know if

I hear anything else."

She ended her call at the same time Dawson was finishing his.

"Well? How did she take it?" she asked.

"She'd diverted her mobile to her workplace phone. A guy answered, said his name was Jack Woodford, her boss. He said she was outside, so I told him what had happened. He said he'd break the news to her gently."

Jo bit her lip and nodded. He would be perfect at that.

WHEN JO ARRIVED back home, her mood hadn't improved at all. She stepped out of the car and slammed the door shut.

"Oh dear. What's happened? Bad day at work?"

She looked over to where Meera was cautiously stepping out of her doorway. She was carrying a cardboard box, neatly labelled 'glassware', and carefully placed it in the open boot of her car.

"I didn't expect to see you here. I thought you'd moved out?"

"I have. I'm just collecting the last few bits and pieces while the boys aren't under my feet. Ben has taken Krish to Helmsley for an ice cream. The removal men seemed very nice, but I felt happier moving some of my more delicate things myself."

"Do you need a hand?" asked Jo.

"No thanks, that was the last box."

Jo sighed. She didn't like being reminded that they weren't neighbours anymore. She recalled what Lucy had said, about her not being one for girly gossiping. Perhaps it was time she changed.

"Have you got time for a chat before you go?" she asked. Meera closed the boot and turned to look at her in surprise, but all she said was: "Always. But I'll have to come to you. There's nowhere to sit here anymore and I've taken the kettle up to the Grange."

Jo opened the cottage door and Meera followed her inside. Knowing she didn't have any teabags and that Meera didn't drink instant coffee, she peered into the fridge and pulled a face.

"Diet Coke?" she offered apologetically.

"Tap water is fine," replied Meera. Relieved that she actually had a clean glass, Jo took the drinks outside and they sat down on the two wooden seats in the garden.

"So?" prompted Meera.

Jo took a deep breath. "I think Jack is seeing Becky."

Meera's eyes opened wide. "Why on earth would you think that?"

"I saw them together the other night in the games room at the pub. He was hugging her."

"Jack hugs everyone. It doesn't mean anything. He's outgoing. A people person. Sometimes I think he should be available on the NHS. I could write out a prescription. *Spend ten minutes in the White Hart with Jack. It's guaranteed to make you feel better.*"

Jo smiled. It was true. He was kind and funny and caring. Maybe she didn't deserve him. She looked up at Meera who was watching her closely.

"Would it upset you if he was seeing her?" she asked gently.

Jo nodded. "You wouldn't believe how much," she said quietly. "But you really don't think there is anything going on between him and Becky?"

Meera shook her head slowly. "No, I don't. I know how he felt about you, and I don't think he's the type to move on that quickly, but you won't know for sure until you speak to him yourself—" she took a sip of her water "—and tell him how you feel."

"I've been an idiot, haven't I?"

Meera gave her a reassuring smile. "You know what Thackeray said: 'Love makes fools of us all.'" She reached over and patted Jo on her shoulder. "It's not too late to do something about it."

JO STARED AT her reflection in the full-length mirror on her bedroom wall. She stood up straight, then yanked down the hem of the one and only little black dress she owned. It had been months since she'd last worn it. She didn't remember it being this short. Her hair was hanging loose around her shoulders, and she had carefully applied mascara and lipstick to her usually bare face. Downstairs there were candles and a bottle of wine on the table. Earlier she'd driven to Thirsk and bought salad, chicken and fresh bread.

After talking to Meera, she'd come up with a plan. She would pull out all the stops. She'd dress up, go to the pub and convince Jack to come home with her. When it was just the two of them, she'd be able to talk to him properly.

Maybe he'd tell her to get lost, but that's a risk she'd have to take. She couldn't remember when she'd last felt this nervous. She didn't think she ever had. Certainly not about a man. She looked in the mirror one last time, wiped a smudge of lipstick off her teeth, took a deep breath and headed out the door.

THE WHITE HART was as busy as ever when Jo stepped through the door. Jack was behind the bar. It was the first time they'd seen each other since that morning with Simon. He looked up and did a double take when he saw her.

"Evening. Where are you off to all dressed up?"

There was no edge in his voice, but no cheeky grin or quip about being ready for a hot date either. He sounded perfectly civil. She hated it. Maybe he didn't care anymore. Meera might be wrong.

"Actually," she began, "I came to see you. I hope you might be able to get away early."

There was a crash from the kitchen. The three old farmers at the bar cheered while Jack winced.

"This isn't a good time, is it?" said Jo.

"Not the best. Mum's gone out to the cinema with Joan. It's just Becky and me tonight."

Jo had to stop herself from flinching. *Becky and me.* It felt like a punch in the stomach, but at least she knew now.

"Just the two of you," she said almost to herself. "I see. I thought so. I mean it makes sense. You've known each other all your lives and you must have been fed up wasting your time on me."

Jack looked up from the pint he was pulling. "What are you on about?"

"You and Becky." She took a deep breath. "I hope she'll make you very happy."

Jack stared at her blankly for a second and then his face broke into a grin. "Becky? Are you serious? She's my best friend's annoying little sister who happens to work here. Nothing more."

Relief and hope surged through her. "Really?"

Jack shook his head, obviously still amused. "She's had a tough time. Of course, I was going to help her if I could. Especially as Rachel twisted my arm. I only wish she could carry more than one plate at a time."

They both watched as the kitchen door swung open and Becky, her face a picture of concentration very slowly and carefully carried a bowl of vegetables across the room and placed it on one of the tables.

"I could help out," Jo suggested, "if you want me to, I mean."

"Seriously?"

"Sure. I waited tables at a bistro in Covent Garden while I was going through college and I've been known to pull the odd pint or two."

Jack gestured to her dress. "What about your hot date?"

Jo ducked round to his side of the bar and fixed him with her sparkling green eyes. "You'll have to wait until later."

Jack stared at her in confusion, but as he opened his mouth the high-pitched wail of a smoke alarm had him heading straight for the kitchen.

BY ELEVEN O'CLOCK, the last few customers were leaving, Jo was wiping down the bar and Becky had already gone home. Between the three of them they'd managed to get through the rest of the evening without any more mishaps. Jack had taken control of the kitchen, while Jo ran the bar and Becky managed not to get in the way too much.

"Phew," gasped Jack as he bolted the door. "What a night! You were great. I don't know how to thank you for stepping in."

Jo looked up at him and smiled. "How about you walk me home?"

THEY MADE THEIR way back to the cottage in silence. Jo was rehearsing in her head what she wanted to say and when she glanced across to Jack, he looked unusually pensive. If he thought it was weird that Miss Independent suddenly needed an escort home, he didn't say anything.

"Wait here for one second," she said when they reached her door. She dashed inside, lit the candles, got the chicken and salad out of the fridge, put on some jazz music she knew Jack liked in the background, then opened the front door with a flourish.

Jack stepped inside, looked around and whistled. "Wow the place looks great. I feel like I should have dressed up.

What's all this in aid of? It's not my birthday, is it?"

Jo took a deep breath. "I wanted to explain about the other day, when you saw Simon leaving. Nothing happened. I swear it didn't. I know it looked that way but..." she began, but Jack interrupted her. His smile had faded.

"It's okay, Jo. You don't have to explain."

"I do. I've treated you badly. You've been really kind to me since I moved here, and I took you for granted. I'm sorry. If I hurt you, I never meant to."

Jack nodded and pointed to the candlelit table. "So that's what all this is? An apology?"

"Yes." She paused and, stepping forward, placed her arms around his neck. "And hopefully a seduction."

THE CHURCH CLOCK was striking midnight and moonlight poured into the room through a narrow gap in the curtains. The little black dress and Jack's rugby shirt lay in a tangled heap on the floor. The salad and wine remained untouched downstairs. Jo sighed and nestled closer to Jack's chest, his arm wrapped tightly around her. She closed her eyes and listened to his breathing. As she felt herself drifting off to sleep. She couldn't remember when she'd felt this happy.

Suddenly, her eyes sprang open again. Somewhere in the room her phone was buzzing. She wriggled free from Jack's hold and sat up. The buzzing was coming from under the bed. She tipped her head over the edge and saw the small screen flashing. It was Dan, Rachel's cousin. She stretched her hand out and grabbed it.

"What's up?" asked Jack sleepily, after she'd finished listening to what Dan had to tell her.

"Max is back, and he's attacked Rachel," replied Jo.

"What? Is she okay?" he asked, immediately sitting up. Jo was already out of bed and pulling her underwear on.

"I think so. Dan and Rob found her. They said she had been hit on the head but is conscious. He's called an ambulance. It looks like Max has been trampled by Rachel's horse. They are all up at some derelict farm on the moors."

"Hold on a second. I'll come with you. You might not find your way there on your own."

"Okay, but hurry up," replied Jo scooping up his clothes and flinging them over to him as she scraped her hair back into a ponytail.

"Is it often going to be like this, being with you?" his muffled voice asked as he pulled on his rugby shirt.

"Probably. Are you up for it?" she asked, smiling over at him.

His head appeared again, his hair sticking up in half a dozen different angles, and he grinned back at her. "Absolutely."

CHAPTER EIGHTEEN

L UCY STOOD AT the window, clutching yet another cup of tea and staring down the driveway. Outside the pale grey light of dawn was slowly creeping over the topiary sculptures that lined the long stretch of gravel. Her phone lay on the windowsill next to her. She'd been waiting for it to ring since seeing Dan and Rob the previous evening.

Freddie had been at cricket practice. It had been delayed a little by the storm. When she'd gone to collect him, he'd been thrilled to tell her that he'd taken his first wicket. He was so excited that before she could stop him, he'd dashed across to the Hayloft where Rob was stepping out of his pickup. She hadn't spoken to him since he'd left abruptly the other night. Feeling rather awkward she went over to them. Rob was nodding and listening intently to Freddie. He looked up and gave her one of his half-smiles.

"It sounds like Yorkshire will be calling him up any day now," he said.

"It does," she agreed. They both turned around at the sound of a noisy diesel engine. A worried-looking Dan Foxton had pulled up in his old Land Rover. He'd asked if either of them had seen Rachel, explaining that she hadn't returned from her ride on the moors. Rob had immediately offered to help look for her.

"I'll let you know if I have any news," he'd promised her. It was only after he'd driven off that Lucy remembered Jo's call about Max possibly being back in the area. She took Freddie home, gave him supper and watched television with him until his bedtime. She wished she could have helped look for her friend too, but she couldn't leave Freddie alone. Joan was out at the cinema and Sadie had disappeared off with the film crew somewhere. Her mother reappeared by eleven and by the look on her face, Lucy assumed the leading man must have turned her down.

As the longcase clock at the bottom of the stairs struck midnight, Lucy grew more and more worried. What if something terrible had happened to Rachel? They had been so close, but she hadn't seen her old friend for days. In truth, she'd been so wrapped up with the estate, Sadie and everything else that she hadn't been a very good friend, and now Rachel could be in trouble. Pointlessly she picked up her phone and checked the screen again.

Through the early morning mist, she suddenly saw the glow of the pickup truck's headlights. She ran down to the courtyard. Rob climbed out of the cab wearily. He looked exhausted and there was a gash on his forehead.

"Thank goodness you're here. I've been so worried. What happened to you?" she asked, rushing forward.

"Sorry I didn't call. There was no signal and then the battery on my phone died."

"Did you find Rachel? Is she okay? What happened to your head?"

"She's fine. During the storm she took refuge in Moorhead Farm, but it turned out Max was hiding out there. He'd run out of money in Spain and come home. He wasn't very happy about being found by his sister-in-law and took a swing at her."

"Oh my God!" gasped Lucy.

"I don't know exactly what happened next, but it looks like her horse gave him a kick. Dan drove home and called Jo. She and Jack came out and she arrested Max. But he and Rachel both needed to go to the hospital. When the others had gone, I stayed behind at the farm to make it secure again. Max had broken the locks to get in. I didn't want anyone else taking advantage, but I was working in the dark and something fell on my head. I think I was knocked out for a couple of minutes too."

"That's terrible. You shouldn't be driving. Shall I take you to the hospital?" she asked ushering him inside.

"No, I'm fine, just a bit knackered."

"At least sit down so I can clean it up," she insisted. He lowered himself on to one of the chairs next to the Aga while she found the first aid box in one of the cupboards.

"Sorry," she whispered as he winced while she wiped the wound with antiseptic. As she lowered her hand, he took hold of her wrist and fixed her with his deep blue eyes.

"Luce, I'm sorry if I've been a bit weird with you."

Normally she would have pretended everything was fine, but as she gazed back at him, she didn't want to pretend anymore. "Was it something I did?"

"No, it wasn't you." He shook his head and winced again. "Can I explain later? I don't think I'll make much sense right now."

"Okay," agreed Lucy. "Look, why don't you crash out here for a few hours."

"Sounds good," replied Rob, yawning widely as he rose to his feet. She led him through to the main hall and pointed up the sweeping staircase.

"There's a bed made up in the blue room. It's the second door on the left at the top of the stairs. Now I know everyone is safe I'm going to check on the marquee after last night's rain. I'll make you some breakfast when I get back."

Lucy watched him trudge upstairs, before returning to the kitchen. She pulled on her coat, whistled for the dogs who were still sniffing around the pickup and headed to the marquee.

Today was the day the Rosemary Centre were holding their fundraising event. Although it wouldn't make the estate any money, Lucy was as eager as ever that everything should run smoothly. She'd been reading about the work the charity did and how many women they had helped over the years. Women who had been frightened and abused by men they thought loved them. She'd shuddered reading their stories, knowing all too well the feelings they described and realising how lucky she was compared to many others. How apt that the event was taking place on the same day that her friend had been attacked by a man she should have been able to trust, her own brother-in-law.

Lucy walked around the edge of the marquee, checking the guide ropes and making sure water hadn't pooled on the roof. When she was sure the rain hadn't caused any damage, she headed back to the kitchen. She found Joan there and quickly filled her in on what had happened to Rachel.

"So, it's been quite a night," she concluded. "Rob is sleeping upstairs. I said I'd make him some breakfast," she said reaching for the frying pan.

Joan gently took it from her. "Why don't you take him a cup of tea and I'll do the breakfast. It sounds like the poor lad has suffered enough."

Lucy pulled an expression of mock outrage before grinning and putting the kettle on to boil. When she'd made the tea, she carefully carried it upstairs, humming to herself. She may have missed out on another night's sleep, but today was going to be a good day. Rachel was okay and it looked like she'd finally find out what had been bothering Rob.

Quietly, she pushed open the bedroom door and froze. Rob wasn't alone in bed. Sadie was under the covers too, her lips hovering above his closed eyes. The cup of tea fell from Lucy's hand and smashed as it hit the floor.

Rob's eyes snapped open. He looked at Sadie in horror, then turned his head towards Lucy.

"Darling! We didn't expect you to be back this early," gasped Sadie sitting up.

Lucy stared at the two of them. If was as if time had slowed down. Her mother was wearing one of her black silk negligees that Lucy had bought to try and win back Rupert's affection but had been stuffed in a drawer for years. Rob's face was creased and crumpled from where it had been pressed against the pillow, his hair was sticking up in several directions and there was sleep in the corners of his eyes.

"Luce, I swear this isn't what it looks like," he stammered.

"I think you should leave," said Lucy coldly.

"Please, Lucy, let me explain," pleaded Rob. "I didn't even know she was here. I opened my eyes and…"

Lucy could feel the hurt and anger building up inside. "Not you. You." She turned and pointed at Sadie, who was staring back at her with wide-eyed innocence.

"Darling, you can't mean that." She pushed her tousled blonde hair away from her face. "You said yourself what an attractive man he is and you weren't in any hurry to make a move. Don't be upset. It was only a bit of fun."

"Just go!"

"But I'm your mother!"

Lucy slowly shook her head as tears filled her eyes. "I don't think you even know what that word means. Pack your things. I'm calling you a taxi."

Without another word, she ran out of the bedroom and down the stairs, ignoring Rob who was shouting her name. When she arrived in the kitchen Joan took one look at her stricken face and hurried over to her.

"Oh my goodness. What's happened, love?"

Lucy was shaking so much she could barely speak as she rested her head against the older woman and tried to steady her breathing. "I need to phone my mother a taxi. I found her in bed with Rob. How could she?"

Joan pursed her lips. "Don't you worry about a taxi. I'll get Bill to drive her to York station. Do you want me to take Freddie down to my place so you can talk to Rob?"

Lucy shook her head. "No, I don't want to talk to him, but please look after Freddie. I can't stay here right now. I'm going to see Rachel."

Gulping back the tears, Lucy drove through the village,

determined to concentrate on the road, but she couldn't get the image of Rob and her mother out of her head. At one point, she thought she might be sick. First, she went to Mary's farmhouse, but the place was in darkness, and for once the back door was locked. When she pulled out of the driveway, she spotted Meera going into Rachel's cottage. Lucy hadn't even realised she'd moved back there. It showed how distant they had become. She parked on the cobbles outside and walked through the front door.

"Hello! It's only me!" she called out.

"We're upstairs," Jo's voice called back. Lucy made her way up the stairs and found a very pale-looking Rachel propped up in bed with Meera peering closely at her heavily bandaged head and Jo sitting opposite them.

"Hello, stranger," said Rachel with a small smile. Her lower lip was bruised and swollen.

"Oh, Rach! That looks really serious. Are you okay?"

"It looks worse than it is. Besides it was worth it to catch Max."

Lucy turned to Jo. "Has he been charged?"

"Yep. I've just been taking her statement, and Mary and Becky are at the station giving theirs," explained Jo. Lucy knew she must not have had very much sleep either, but she looked surprisingly bright-eyed.

"I feel okay now. I really think I should be with them," said Rachel sounding groggy as she tried to sit up a little higher.

"No," replied Meera firmly, "you need plenty of rest. They will be okay. Dan drove them to Northallerton and will bring them back again and they can tell you everything that happened then."

"But who's looking after Minty?"

"She's with Shirley and Jack, being spoilt rotten," Jo assured her.

"And Mary and Becky are both stronger than you think," added Lucy, reaching out and giving her friend's hand a squeeze.

"Maybe," said Rachel slightly reluctantly, then frowned up at her.

"You don't look too great either. What's up?"

Lucy felt herself flush as Jo and Meera turned to inspect her too. She may as well get it over with.

"I caught my mum in bed with Rob."

"What!" exclaimed the other three in unison. Rachel's sleepy eyes were wide open now.

"When you say in bed. Were they actually, you know…" Rachel trailed off and Lucy shook her head.

"No, not exactly. Rob said he was asleep when she climbed in next to him."

"Then maybe you shouldn't be too hard on him," suggested Meera gently.

"Maybe not, but no matter how hard I try, I can't get the image of her next to him out of my head."

"Bloody hell! I knew I should have said something!" exclaimed Jo. She threw up her hands in outrage.

"What do you mean?" asked Lucy.

"Your mother has been trying to get her claws into Rob for ages, ever since she found out he's loaded," Jo continued pointing Rachel and Meera. "I knew I shouldn't have listened to you two about families. I've always said they're more trouble than they're worth."

"I don't think all this excitement is good for Rachel. Perhaps we could all do with a nice cup of tea. I'll go and make it. Jo, will you help me?" Meera said, standing up and giving Jo a meaningful look.

When the other two had left the room, Rachel and Lucy sat in silence for a few minutes, listening to Jo complaining and Meera placating quietly downstairs.

"What did you say when you found them?" asked Rachel finally.

Lucy shrugged. "Not much. I kicked Sadie out."

"Are you okay?"

"Yes," she replied, "or at least I will be. Let's face it, I've managed most of my life without her."

"What about Rob?"

"I don't know. Maybe this is for the best. I mean, I liked him a lot. I even thought we might have a future together. He's been really kind and helpful." Lucy sighed. "But maybe I was in danger of falling into the trap of relying on another man too much. That's always been my problem. Like mother like daughter, I suppose."

"You shouldn't be so tough on yourself. All these weddings and the filming. You organised them. It's you who's held everything together, and you shouldn't be so tough on Rob either. He's a good guy."

They lapsed into silence again. Lucy looked around the room. Above Rachel's bed was the map of the world. She had intended to cover it with pins whenever she visited somewhere new, but so far there were only a handful. The most recent was stuck in the middle of Italy.

"What happened with Sarah? I thought she would be here," she asked.

Rachel looked away. "Things didn't work out," she replied.

"Why not? When she said she'd left South America early to surprise you in Italy, I thought it sounded terribly romantic."

"It was. Nobody has ever done anything like that for me." Rachel closed her eyes and sighed. "It was a pity I had to come home and clear up Max's mess."

"Isn't she still working here in Hartwell? I thought she was extending the Druid burial site."

"Yes, she is. It's a real passion of hers. She actually made me think Hartwell might not be as dull as I had imagined. We even talked about her staying here at the cottage at least part of the time. We were getting on really well, but…" Rachel trailed off again. "Then she found all the photos I had of you. I tried to explain, but she was really upset. Then all this happened. Like you said, maybe it's for the best. Who could blame her for not wanting to be involved in all this drama?"

Lucy wished she could think of something helpful or comforting to say, but at that moment, Meera and Jo returned with a tray of tea and a plate of buttered scones.

"Shirley popped in to drop these off. She's baked them specially this morning and said she'd call in and see you later and to tell you Minty is very happily playing with Baxter," said Meera handing out the mugs of tea.

"There are about half a dozen Tupperware boxes full of cakes and pies down there too. I think your family are making sure you don't starve," added Jo.

"All my aunties are feeders. I'll be the size of a house by the time I'm allowed out of bed," groaned Rachel as she tentatively sipped her tea.

Jo cleared her throat. She looked unusually flushed. "Since you're all here, I thought I should tell you Jack and I are together."

"That's wonderful!" gasped Meera reaching over to give Jo a hug.

"That's why he was with you last night!" exclaimed Lucy.

Jo nodded. She couldn't stop smiling. All three of them turned to look at Rachel.

"I'm very happy for you, but if you hurt him again, I'll kill you."

Jo shrugged good-naturedly. "I wouldn't expect anything less, Rach."

"It seems like a long time since the four of us have been together like this. I've missed it," said Meera.

Rachel attempted a weak smile. "Perhaps I should get bashed on the head more often."

"You shouldn't joke about that sort of thing," Meera chided, her face serious. "Head injuries can be very dangerous."

Lucy picked up a scone but put it straight down again. She really didn't have an appetite. "How are the plans for the village fete coming along?" she asked.

Meera's face immediately brightened. "Really well. Caroline is in charge, so as you can imagine everybody is doing as they are told. In fact, I received a text from her on my way over here. She said she is putting Ben in charge of the duck race. I assume that's because he's a vet. But I don't really understand how they train the ducks to race. To be honest, it sounds a little bit cruel."

Lucy couldn't help herself. She burst into a fit of giggles. "Meera! That's priceless! It's usually me who says something stupid."

She continued to laugh at Meera's confused expression as Rachel, who was also grinning lopsidedly, patiently explained that they used yellow plastic ducks. "You know like the ones you had in the bath when you were little."

"What? I never had ducks in the bath, did you?" Meera, looking even more perplexed, turned to Jo for support.

She shook her head. "I really didn't have that kind of childhood, Meera," she replied cheerfully.

"Sorry, Meera," Lucy apologised wiping the tears from her eyes, "but thank you. After this morning, I didn't imagine I'd ever laugh again."

"Well, I'm pleased I cheered you up," replied Meera, then she glanced across to Rachel. "I think we should probably leave you in peace. Let you get some rest."

"You do look terrible," agreed Jo, downing the last of her tea and shoving another scone into her mouth.

"Thanks a lot," muttered Rachel.

Lucy gave Rachel one last hug goodbye before following Meera and Jo downstairs and out of the cottage.

"I bet it felt good slapping those handcuffs on Max," she said.

"It was extremely satisfying," replied Jo with a wry smile. "I was a bit surprised when you said Mary was giving a statement. I didn't think she wanted to press charges."

"That was before Max attacked her daughter. I always had her down as the meek and mild type, but she looked fairly ferocious when I saw her at the station."

"Yeh, Rachel and Becky are lucky. She's an amazing mother," agreed Lucy, her mind drifting back to her own less than perfect parent. Meera and Jo exchanged a look.

"Are you going back to sort things out with Rob?" asked Meera.

"You should at least give him a chance to explain," added Jo, but Lucy shook her head.

"Not yet. I'm going to drive through to York. There's something I need to do there."

THE UNIVERSITY CAMPUS was much bigger than she had expected, and it took her half an hour to even find the archaeology department. Then she had to trail along endless corridors and up countless flights of stairs until she found herself outside a door bearing the name *Dr Sarah Stevenson*. Lucy raised her hand and knocked.

"Come in," called out a clear voice.

Lucy took a deep breath, opened the door, stepped inside and switched on her brightest smile. "Hello, I don't know if you remember me. I'm Lucy Hanley, a friend of Rachel's," she began.

Sarah looked up at her. A flicker of surprise crossed her face. "Yes. I know who you are. How can I help?" She sounded brisk and polite, but her smile didn't quite reach to her eyes.

"Rachel was attacked last night. By Max, her brother-in-law. The one we thought was in Spain. It turned out he came back. He was hiding in an empty farmhouse up on the moors."

Lucy was aware that her words were tumbling out and she wasn't making much sense as Sarah stared at her incredulously.

"What? Is she all right?"

"Yes, she's back at home now. Her cottage, not the farmhouse. She was bashed on the head. She needed stitches, but she's okay. Well, a bit groggy. I thought you would like to know." She paused. "And you might want to go and see her."

Sarah seemed to be studying her hands before finally looking up. "Thank you. I'm pleased you told me, but I think if she wanted to see me, she would have contacted me herself. I take it she didn't ask you to come here."

"No," admitted Lucy. "She doesn't know I'm here. Look, I know you were upset when you found some photos of me, but they didn't mean anything, not really and... Oh dear, I'm not expressing myself very well. I didn't get much sleep and driving over here I thought I'd be able to explain everything to you, but I'm just talking nonsense."

"It's all right. I know nothing happened between you and Rachel, but it doesn't change the fact she has feelings for you."

"Had. That's all in the past. And even if things were different, I wouldn't have been right for Rachel. She needs someone like you. Someone wise and clever, someone who can support her, the way she supports everyone else. Because that's what she does. That's all she's been doing for months. Putting everyone else first, taking care of us. Me, her mum, her sister, even her dad, before he died. If she were a selfish sort of person, she would have gone to South America with you or stayed in Italy, but that isn't who she is. She's loyal and kind and caring."

"I know all that," said Sarah quietly.

"But what she isn't good at, what she's rubbish at, in fact, is asking for help. She keeps all her problems and worries to herself. She thinks she would be burdening you if she shared them."

Sarah shook her head. "That's not how a relationship should work. Look, Lucy, I like Rachel a lot, but there were simply too many alarm bells ringing and working up here on the fourth floor, I've learnt that the safe thing to do when the alarm sounds is to get out."

"Really? At my house it usually only means I've burnt the toast again," joked Lucy hoping humour might help, but Sarah didn't look amused and something in her expression made Lucy pause. Here she was begging Sarah to give Rachel another chance, to go against her instincts, yet she wasn't prepared to do the same for Rob, when Meera and Jo had told her to.

"Well thanks for listening and not kicking me out," she said finally, but Sarah merely raised her hand in response.

Lucy left the university shaking her head. Coming here had been a mistake. She had really wanted to help Rachel, to help make things right between her and Sarah, but when her own life was such a mess maybe she shouldn't be interfering in the lives of others. She drove back to Hartwell with the radio on loud, but the pop music couldn't block out the voices in her head. Rob protesting his innocence. Sadie doing the same. Jo furious with Sadie on her behalf. As she passed the railway station, she hoped Bill had done as Joan promised and put Sadie on the first train back to London.

It was ironic, she thought. All those times as a little girl she'd pleaded with Sadie not to leave following one of her brief visits. She could vividly remember being about six years old, standing on her bedroom windowsill, tears streaming down her face, hammering her little fist against the glass as Sadie swept down the street on the arm of her latest boyfriend without a backward glance. Now she was praying that she was long gone. The only question was had Rob left too.

He hadn't. When she returned to Hartwell Hall, she found him sitting on the wall by the back door. He was still wearing the clothes he'd had on from the night before, his face looked pale beneath his tan and dried blood was still clumped in his hair. Lucy's heart lurched as soon as she saw him. He looked up at her with lined, tired eyes.

"What are you doing here?" she asked.

"Waiting for you. I know you might not want to see me right now, but I need to explain. I promise nothing happened between me and Sadie. I woke up a second before you walked in. I was as shocked as you were. It's true I've shared a drink with her in the pub, but it was because I wanted to talk about you. I really like you, but I didn't want to rush you. Sadie offered to give me some advice. I've been going over things in my head and I really don't think I ever gave Sadie any reason to think that I would want her to do that. If I did, I'm really sorry."

Lucy stared at him for a moment. "I think that's the most you've ever said to me."

He gave a wry smile and shook his head. "Well, I should have said more. A lot more. I should have been talking to you instead of listening to Sadie. She told me you were worried about me having been in prison. She said to give you space, so I did. That's why I might have seemed a bit off-hand, but…"

Lucy stepped forward and gently placed her fingers against his lips to silence him.

"It's all right. I know it was Sadie not you. Jo told me she'd been after you for a while, but I think I knew what she was really like myself, deep down. She will never be the mother I wanted her to be. I've accepted that. Now I think you should go back to the Hayloft."

He looked at her in bewilderment. "But you just said you believed me."

"I do, but you can't take me to the charity reception dressed like that. You need to go home, shower and change." She glanced at her watch. "Preferably in less than twenty minutes."

Rob's face suddenly broke into a smile. "You still want me to go with you?"

"You don't get out of it that easily."

He suddenly pulled her towards him and kissed her on the lips. She allowed herself to kiss him back for a few seconds before playfully pushing him away with a grin.

"The clock's ticking."

"I'm on my way," he replied, dropping another kiss on top of her head, before climbing into his pickup.

CHAPTER NINETEEN

"LOOK AT YOU, Meera. You look like the lady of the manor."

Meera smoothed down her new floral-print shift dress, then adjusted the brim of her large straw hat. Standing behind her was her mother, smiling proudly back at her reflection.

"You don't think the hat makes me look even shorter?"

"No, no, it is very elegant. And I can't remember when I last saw you looking this happy. Also, you are not short, you are petite," her mother reassured her.

Meera smiled back at her mother who was at least two inches shorter than herself.

It was the day of the village fete and she had invited her parents to come and stay for the weekend. After weeks of prevaricating, she had decided to kill not two, but three birds with one stone. While they thought they would be spending the weekend at the cottage, Meera had convinced Nish to drive them to the Grange instead. She and Ben had stood side by side on the front steps, waiting to greet them. Feeling sick with nerves, she'd announced this was her new home. While they were still stunned from this news, she'd introduced them to Ben. Then he and Nish had taken Krish outside so she could drop her third bombshell. She had sat them down in the drawing room and explained that she was divorcing Dev and the reason why.

For several minutes they had sat on the sofa, surrounded by half-unpacked boxes, staring blankly back at her. Their faces frozen in shock. Meera held her breath. She knew they had very traditional views on just about everything. She braced herself for an outburst of anger or disappointment, maybe they would even plead with her to change her mind, but they remained silent. Then to Meera's horror, tears filled her father's eyes and began to roll down his face. Slowly, he had risen to his feet and walked out of the room.

"Daddy!" she cried and jumped up to chase after him.

Her mother had reached out and grabbed hold of her arm. "Let him go, Meera," she said softly. "He needs a moment. He will blame himself for all this. Why didn't you tell us before?"

"I couldn't. I knew how disappointed and shocked you would be, and I promised Dev. If I'd told you, his family might have found out too."

"He shouldn't have lied, and he shouldn't have encouraged you to lie to us either."

"He was scared. He's always been scared," replied Meera, remembering Nish's reaction when she'd told him about Dev.

"I still can't believe it. We hardly hear from you all summer and then you drop this bombshell on our heads. And I can't believe you told Nish before you told us," continued her mother. The colour had returned to her face and the hint of indignation in her voice told Meera that she was getting over the initial shock.

"Don't be angry with him. He's been great these last few weeks. A really supportive brother."

"Well, it's about time," tutted her mother.

"Will Daddy be okay?"

Her mother stood up and, taking Meera's face in her hands, she rose on to her tiptoes and kissed her on the forehead. "He'll be fine. All we have ever both wanted is for you to be happy."

MEERA FINALLY FOUND her father outside. He was leaning against Nish's car, with his arms folded, staring back at the Grange. Meera went and silently stood by his side.

"This is a nice place you have found," he said finally without looking at her. "It is like one of those places in all those books you used to read when you were a girl. Your head was always buried in a book. Your mother was worried you would ruin your eyesight." He paused and turned to look at her. "And this man you have found—Ben. Is he a good man?"

"Oh yes, Daddy. He is. He's kind and clever and he loves Krish and me very much. He would do anything for us."

"It seems you have created a good future for yourself. You have done a better job than I did."

"What happened with Dev isn't your fault. On paper he seemed to be perfect. I was very happy to marry him."

"You were always happy to do as I asked. Now it's my turn to do as you ask. If you want it, you have my blessing for this new life you are making."

Meera flung her arms around him in relief. "Thank you, Daddy. Of course I want your blessing. I've only ever wanted you to be proud of me."

Her father hugged her back tightly. "How could I be anything else?" he said softly.

THAT EVENING, AFTER supper, Ben and her father sat out on the terrace talking intently, while Krish watched cartoons with Nish. Meera showed her mother around the house and tried to explain what would be happening at the village fete the next day, but she found the idea of the duck race just as puzzling as her daughter. It was late when they all finally went to bed. Meera switched off the light and snuggled up to Ben, sighing contentedly. She could hardly believe that all the people she loved most in the world were sleeping under one roof and there were no more secrets between them.

"Relieved it's over?" asked Ben softly in her ear.

"Very," replied Meera.

"I told you not to worry."

"You and Dad seemed to be having a good chat."

"It was a bit more like an interrogation than a chat, but yes, I think it went okay. Your mother still seems a bit disappointed that I'm not a doctor though. She cheered up a bit when I told her I had a PhD in bovine dentistry."

Meera chuckled. "Well, be prepared that from now on she will always refer to you as 'my daughter's partner Dr Ben Bannister' especially when she is introducing you to her friends."

"I can live with that," he whispered back as he planted a kiss on top of her head. Meera was still smiling when she closed her eyes and fell into a deep sleep.

THE NEXT MORNING, the committee members arrived early to start setting up the stalls. Meera was determined to be the most gracious of hostesses and wandered amongst them handing out mugs of tea and coffee, as well as freshly baked Danish pastries. She had introduced her parents to Caroline, who was ordering everyone around including Nish. He had been roped in to help Jack assemble a small marquee that would be used as the beer tent.

Meera paused and watched them for a moment. It felt strange having her brother in Hartwell, almost like an anachronism, as if she was watching *Pride and Prejudice* and Mr Darcy suddenly produced a phone from his waistcoat pocket. Since that night in Harrogate, she'd started to appreciate Nish more. For years they had been distant, barely communicating except for the odd sniping comment, but if it hadn't been for him, they would never have caught the man threatening her child and, who knows, maybe she wouldn't even have had the strength to start divorce proceedings.

The previous day's post had brought news from Dev, or rather his solicitors. Keen to keep things amicable, she'd phoned him to thank him and ask if he wanted to arrange a time to talk to Krish about the divorce.

"I thought it might be better if you explained everything to him," he'd replied.

"I have, but don't you want to come here and talk to him yourself?"

"I would love to, Meera, but I'm going to be out of the country for a few weeks. I need to take some time after everything I've been through."

"Are you going back to India?"

"No. Australia."

"Australia!" exclaimed Meera.

"Yes. Liam got in touch with me. He'd heard about what Darren tried to do and he wanted to apologise. It was really very sweet of him. Anyway, we got talking and he invited me to go and visit him over there."

It was on the tip of Meera's tongue to berate him, but instead she took a deep breath.

"That sounds wonderful, Dev. I hope it all goes well for you."

"Thanks, Meera. Now I must dash. My taxi has arrived. Give Krish my love. Tell him I'll bring him a great present back from Oz."

However, Meera hadn't spoken to Krish about his father being out of the country. The weekend was going well, and she didn't want anything to spoil it.

As usual, Caroline was going to open the fete, but she had asked Meera and Ben to join her so she could publicly thank them on behalf of the committee. Meera was desperate to be on time, but Ben was already five minutes late. Suddenly she saw him hurrying across the lawn towards her. His glasses were skew-whiff and there were several tent pegs dangling from his hand.

"Don't you think you should have changed?" she asked, as together they headed down the drive to where Caroline was waiting.

"Why? What's wrong with what I'm wearing?" he asked, looking down at the old pair of shorts with a hole in them and a T-shirt that was spotted with grease from the bacon sandwich he'd had for breakfast.

"It's not very smart."

"I don't need to be smart. I'll be down by the stream for the duck race most of the day. I'll probably end up getting soaked."

The entrance to the Grange's driveway had been decorated with balloons and bunting, and there was a thin piece of rope draped across with a hand-painted sign reading 'Hartwell Fete' hanging from it. Meera began to feel a little nervous when she saw the crowd on the other side of the rope, all waiting. Suddenly she spotted Lucy smiling and waving at her. Rob had his arm around her waist and Freddie was sitting on his shoulders. Meera waved back, then quickened her pace when she noticed Caroline giving them a meaningful look as she tapped her watch.

"Best get a move on," whispered Ben, taking her hand.

Caroline turned to the crowd as they arrived by her side. "On behalf of the Hartwell Fete Committee, I should like to thank Mr Bannister and Dr Kumar for stepping in at short notice—" she glared at Lucy "—and offering us the use of their beautiful new home. I should like to call upon them to officially open this year's Hartwell Fete."

With a flourish she handed Meera a fearsome pair of garden shears. Ben and Meera took a handle each and rather awkwardly, after three attempts, finally cut through the rope to loud applause. The crowd began swarming down the drive and into the garden.

IT WAS LATE in the afternoon and the fete was drawing to a close. As far as Meera could see as she wandered around, it had been a huge success. The rain she had been worrying about all week had failed to materialise; in fact there was barely a cloud in the sky. Children were trying to cool down by paddling in the stream as they ate ice creams before going home. Nora, who was in charge of the white elephant stall, was haggling with Reverend Davenport, who wanted ten pence knocking off a crocheted tea cosy. Rachel, who looked much better than Meera had expected, told her that the tombola had taken a record amount but had now run out of prizes. Joan, who was beginning to wilt along with few remaining blooms on the plant stall she had been running with Bill, managed to give her a friendly wave. Rob was fixing some bunting that had fallen down by the main gate.

Nish had surprised her by not sloping off to the beer tent and was instead helping Becky and Araminta run the lucky dip. He didn't even seem to mind that his expensive trainers were covered in sawdust. Her mother had been thrilled to win the duck race and was proudly carrying around her trophy. Her father had barely left the cake tent and she was sure he must have sampled every bun and cupcake they had to offer. The only person she couldn't see anywhere was Ben.

"Have you seen Ben?" she asked Jo, who was collecting empty plastic glasses from the tables outside the beer tent.

"He was talking to your dad and then he drove off with Lucy about quarter of an hour ago."

"Lucy? Oh dear, I hope none of her dogs are poorly," said Meera with a frown. She decided to take another tour of the garden and start collecting any rubbish that may have been left behind. When she returned to the beer tent, the place was deserted, and it looked like almost everyone had left. Krish came running over.

"Mum! Ben's in the house and needs to talk to you."

"What about?" asked Meera, but her son had disappeared as quickly as he'd arrived. With a sigh, she put down her sack of litter and walked over to the house.

As SHE STEPPED through the front door into the hallway, she could hear classical music playing somewhere. Mozart's violin concerto it sounded like. She must have forgotten to turn the radio off. She followed the music into the drawing room and stopped abruptly. The curtains had been drawn across all the windows and instead the room was lit with long tapering candles. Standing in front of the fireplace was Ben. At least it looked like Ben, but now he was dressed immaculately in a Victorian outfit complete with frock coat and breeches.

"Ben! What is all this?" she gasped.

Ben adjusted his glasses self-consciously and cleared his throat.

"Meera, whatever our souls are made of, yours and mine are the same. I offer you my hand and my heart."

Meera's hand flew to her mouth. He was quoting the Brontës to her. The next moment, he dropped down on one knee and produced a sparkling sapphire and diamond ring.

"Will you marry me?"

Meera nodded dumbly, her eyes filling with tears of happiness. Ben's serious face broke into a smile of relief as he took her hand and slipped on the ring.

"I thought you deserved a proper proposal. Something more memorable than a quick chat in your consulting room."

"It was perfect. Thank you," she said softly.

"Are you sure? Because I actually wrote a lot more." He fished out a crumpled sheet of paper from his pocket. "I went through all your favourite books, picking out the best bits. I've got some Austen here too and even some Hardy. There's a good bit about sitting by the fire and looking up. Would you like to hear it?"

She reached up and silenced him with a long kiss. "It was perfect," she assured him, before turning her head. "Where is that music coming from?"

Ben raised a finger to his lips and beckoned her over to the large cupboard in the corner. He pushed open the folding door to reveal Nish, who jumped and immediately put down the violin.

"Oh, my goodness!" gasped Meera.

"You did say I should have kept playing," replied Nish, smiling at her shocked face. He removed two lumps of cotton wool from his ears. "I didn't want to have to hear the mushy stuff," he explained.

"What's happening? Did she say yes?" shouted a voice from out in the hall.

"Is that Daddy?" asked Meera.

"Yes," replied Ben, looking a little embarrassed. "He's waiting outside with Krish and your mum."

"They all knew what you were planning?"

"Of course. I had to do the right thing and ask his permission first—and Krish's."

"Can we come in yet?" Meera heard her son shout from outside.

"Yes," Ben shouted back.

Krish came careering through the door and threw his arms around Ben and Meera. Meera's parents followed at a slightly more sedate pace, but both were smiling broadly. They kissed her and her father shook Ben's hand.

"Congratulations and welcome to our family."

"I can't believe you all knew about this," said Meera, wiping the tears from her eyes.

"Not just us," said Nish, pulling back the heavy curtains at the window. Standing out on the terrace were Jo, Rachel, Lucy, Jack, Rob and Freddie. Nish opened the door.

"Well?" demanded Jack, who was brandishing a bottle of champagne.

"She said yes!" Ben replied with a grin. He took Meera's hand and led her outside as their friends began clapping cheering. Jack shook the bottle so vigorously the cork flew out and everyone was drenched with champagne. Rachel and Lucy squealed as they grabbed some glasses.

"You all knew?" repeated Meera, who felt like she was in a dream.

"Where do you think Ben got his costume from?" Lucy laughed.

"And the violin," added Nish.

Meera looked at them all in confusion.

"Lucy took me back to Hartwell Hall and we raided the film company's prop department," explained Ben.

"I can't believe it," murmured Meera.

Rachel grinned as she handed Meera a glass of champagne. "Come on, Meera, you know how good we are at keeping secrets here in Hartwell," she said, raising her glass. "To Ben and Meera."

"To Ben and Meera," echoed the others.

CHAPTER TWENTY

R ACHEL LAY DOWN on the grass and stretched out her arm to fish the last stray plastic duck out of the weeds in the stream. It was the day after the fete. All thoughts of clearing up had disappeared in the excitement of celebrating Meera and Ben's engagement the previous evening. The committee members and a few others had returned the next morning to pack away and tidy the Grange gardens.

Rachel added the dripping duck to the others in her bucket, then propped herself up and watched everyone else busy at work. As usual Caroline was firmly in charge of proceedings. The colonel offered advice and encouragement as Rob and Jack dismantled the marquee where the teas and cakes had been served. Krish was introducing Minty to Darwin. Her mother was piling up the empty plates and Tupperware boxes from the cake stall for Becky and Nish to carry back to the car.

It was impossible to say which of her old friends looked happier: Jack who hadn't stopped grinning since he finally got together with Jo, or Meera who had seemingly overnight developed a habit of using her left hand to point and gesture at every opportunity. She was wafting serenely along in a floaty dress, directing Ben and Jo who were moving the plant pots and garden urns back into position.

Naturally not everyone had been happy for Ben and Meera. Nora had taken great delight in repeating several times that she didn't see how someone could get engaged if they were still married.

"Talk about putting the cart before the horses," she'd tutted.

Rachel lay back on the grass and closed her eyes. She still felt a little weak and she was in no hurry to be given another task by Caroline. Maybe she could simply rest here for a while and enjoy the last of the summer sun. It was another hot, still day. Probably one of the last they would enjoy this year. The crops had all been harvested and soon the fields would be ploughed ready to be drilled with seed again. In a little over a week, school would begin, and the leaves of the trees would turn to gold and brown. Her hand went to her neck and fiddled with the ancient coin hanging on a chain there. A shadow fell across her face.

"You never did show me the Hartwell noble. I was beginning to think they didn't really exist."

Rachel opened her eyes and squinted. For a second, she thought she might be hallucinating; but no, Sarah really was smiling down at her.

"How are you?" she asked gently.

Rachel staggered to her feet. "I'm fine. What are you doing here? I mean it's good to see you, but..." She paused, frightened of saying the wrong thing.

"I got word that funding for my research into the Druids of Hartwell has been approved."

"That's fantastic. Congratulations!"

"Thanks. I also had a visit from Lucy. She came to tell me that nothing had ever happened between the two of you and what a wonderful person you are, but I already knew that."

"You did?"

Sarah nodded. "I suppose all I need is to know how you feel about me."

Rachel reached out and gently placed her hands on either side of Sarah's face, staring into her beautiful brown eyes. "I think you're amazing. And you didn't just make me fall in love with you. You even got me to fall in love with Hartwell again. For the first time in years, I didn't want to run away. I wanted to stay here. Stay here with you."

Their lips met and when Sarah pulled away, she looked serious. "From now on let's make a deal. No more secrets. I know you love being independent and I love that about you too, but I'd like to be included in your life. All of it. Your family, your friends the village, everything. Deal?"

"Deal," agreed Rachel, letting her hands fall and silently crossing her fingers behind her back. There were some secrets she could never share. A smile spread across Sarah's face.

"You know, the dig starts again after the bank holiday. My car is parked in the village. It's loaded up with stuff…"

"Then we'd better go home and unpack."

THAT EVENING JACK had decided to extend the engagement celebrations by throwing a party for Ben and Meera in the White Hart. He'd drafted in Dan, the colonel and some of the other members of the cricket team to help. Sarah and Rachel walked through the door hand in hand, ignoring Nora's loud exclamation of: "What is the world coming to?"

They found a seat out in the garden. It was the same place they'd sat when Sarah had arrived from Naples.

"You stay here," instructed Sarah. "I'll go and get us some drinks."

Rachel watched her go. She couldn't quite believe she was here. Looking around the garden she spotted most of her friends and family. Jack had set up his old decks and found some flashing disco lights that he'd dotted around the edge of a makeshift wooden dance floor. He was now acting as DJ with Jo perched on a stool next to him flicking through his record collection and teasing him about his taste in music. Lucy and Rob had their arms wrapped around each other as they swayed in time to the beat. When Jo spotted Rachel, she slipped off the stool and made her way over. With a beer in one hand and her hair hanging loose, she looked the picture of contentment.

"You're looking very happy," she said as she approached Rachel's table.

"So, are you," replied Rachel. "Things going well between you and Jack?"

"Things are great. Apart from his terrible taste in music. If he doesn't stop playing Oasis, I might have to scream." She laughed.

Rachel gave her a sidelong glance. "No more visitors from London?"

Jo folded her arms across her chest, suddenly defensive. "No and I don't expect any. Simon was never interested in me, only in what I could tell him about Rupert's guns."

Rachel sat up a little straighter and lowered her voice. "He was here asking about Rupert? What did he want to know?"

Jo merely shrugged. "It sounds like Rupert sold his guns for drugs and they wound up getting used in an armed robbery."

"Have you told Lucy?"

"No, why worry her? Simon is only really interested in securing a conviction for two London gangsters." Jo looked over to Lucy who was shouting out requests to Jack. "I'd better get back to them. Her taste in music is even worse than his."

Rachel prayed her friend's instincts were correct. It had been weeks since she'd dreamt about Rupert. She'd hoped she could finally put that particular chapter of her life behind her. As Jo returned to Jack, she noticed her mother was standing with Joan and Shirley on the edge of the dance floor. Huddled together they were deep in conversation.

"You three are looking very furtive," she called over. "Like the witches in *Macbeth*."

The three older women looked around in surprise.

"Be careful or we'll hex you," retorted Shirley with a quick grin.

Mary left the other two and came over to give Rachel a hug. "I didn't know you were here. How are you feeling, love?"

"I'm fine, Mum. What were you three plotting?"

"Plotting? Don't be silly. You know how we love to gossip and there's plenty to talk about at the moment. Lucy kicking Sadie out, Ben and Meera's engagement, and Jo and

Jack finally getting together." Mary nodded over to where Jo was attempting to get Jack to change the record. "They seem very happy. Do you think she has changed her mind about staying here?"

"I don't know. Jack is always saying her Hartwell noble means she belongs here; maybe he's finally convinced her. Why?"

"No reason really. I think we all expected her to return to London, that's all." Her face clouded for a second, before breaking into a smile again. "You know how Shirley will worry about Jack getting hurt, or worse still moving down there too." Her eyes strayed over Rachel's head. "My goodness, is that Sarah? Is she back?"

Rachel glanced over her shoulder. Sarah was slowly making her way through the throng of people, a glass in each hand.

"Yes, she is. For good this time, I think."

Mary smiled down at her. "I'm very pleased for you, love, and I'll leave you to it." She turned to go. "By the way, after all the excitement about Max, you never actually told me how you got the photos of him meddling with my oven."

Rachel felt herself flush. "Sorry, Mum, I should have said. We couldn't work out what was going on with you, so Meera, Jo and I thought it would be a good idea to put a camera in the kitchen. I know it was a bit sneaky, but it was for your own good and I promise to take it down when I'm feeling better."

Mary put her hands on her hips and pretended to look offended.

"Huh! For my own good indeed! And you accuse me and my friends of plotting and being secretive."

Rachel watched her mother return to Joan and Shirley, then gave a quick wave to Meera and Ben who were chatting to Becky and Nish. She smiled up at Sarah, as she set the two glasses of wine down on the table. To a loud protest from Jo and a cheer from Lucy, Jack suddenly changed the track for Abba's 'Dancing Queen'. Rob led Lucy on to the dance floor, while Jack picked up a laughing Jo and began twirling her around.

"Do you want to join them?" Sarah asked nodded towards the dancing couples.

"Maybe another time," Rachel replied with a smile. "I'm not sure I'm up to strutting my stuff just yet."

Sarah sat down and looked at her with concern. "Are you sure you're okay having a drink? Are you taking any pain medication for your head? Will it react with it?"

"One won't hurt," Rachel assured her as she took a sip of red wine. She wasn't used to anyone fussing over her, but she had to admit it she quite liked it. They sat in silence for a moment, watching the party unfold.

"Do you think Nish is flirting with Becky?" asked Rachel nodding towards where her sister was sitting beneath an apple tree, laughing at something he was saying. Sarah studied them for a moment.

"Yes definitely," she replied decisively, then seeing Rachel's disapproving expression, she nudged her playfully. "Oh come on. She deserves a bit of fun, and he can't be too bad if he's Meera's brother. By the way, you still haven't told me what's happening with Max."

"He started denying everything at first, trying to blame Becky, but when the charges began piling up, especially the assault charge against me, he changed his mind and decided to change his pleas to guilty. I think he's hoping it will reduce his sentence."

"At least that might mean your sister and mother won't be called to give evidence against him, but he deserves to be locked up for what he did. Especially for attacking you. He could have killed you," said Sarah with a slight shudder.

Automatically Rachel's hand went to the back of her head where Max had struck her. The stitches had been removed, but it still felt sore. Thinking about Max reminded her of the village in Italy where she'd received Meera's phone call and first discovered her brother-in-law's betrayal. That place and its inhabitants had reminded her so much of Hartwell. For years she'd been trying to get away from the village, believing it was holding her back in some way, causing her problems. Now she felt quite differently.

She rested her head against Sarah's shoulder. What she'd said at the Grange was true. Thanks to her, Rachel had begun to see her village in a different way. It could be friendly and fun, serious and secretive. It was the place where all those she was closest to lived. Not only her family, but also Meera, Jack, Jo and Lucy and now Sarah. Hopefully the two of them had plenty of holidays and trips abroad ahead of them, but she now knew she would always return to Hartwell.

THE END

Don't miss the next book in The Secrets of Hartwell series, *Four Silences Broken*!

Join Tule Publishing's newsletter for more great reads and weekly deals!

Acknowledgements

My thanks as always to the wonderful team at Tule: Jane Porter, Meghan Farrell, Cyndi Parent and Nikki Babri.

I was very lucky to work with three amazing editors again: Sinclair Sawhney, Helena Newton and Marlene Roberts. Many thanks for all your suggestions and your support.

A big thank you also to Lee Hyat for coordinating the beautiful book cover design.

If you enjoyed *Four Secrets Kept,*
you'll love the next book in...

The Secrets of Hartwell series

Book 1: *Four Hidden Treasures*

Book 2: *Four Secrets Kept*

Book 3: *Four Silences Broken*

Available now at your favorite online retailer!

More Books by H L Marsay

The Chief Inspector Shadow series

Book 1: *A Long Shadow*

Book 2: *A Viking's Shadow*

Book 3: *A Ghostly Shadow*

Book 4: *A Roman Shadow*

Book 5: *A Forgotten Shadow*

Book 6: *A Christmas Shadow*

Available now at your favorite online retailer!

About the Author

H L Marsay always loved detective stories and promised herself that one day, she would write one too. She is lucky enough to live in York, a city full of history and mystery. When not writing, the five men in her life keep her busy – two sons, two dogs and one husband.

Thank you for reading

Four Secrets Kept

If you enjoyed this book, you can find more from all our great authors at TulePublishing.com, or from your favorite online retailer.

TULE
PUBLISHING

Printed in Great Britain
by Amazon

30913403R00152